I could see Stu's shadowed face looking down
at the piano keys. I wondered if he were
making up the words as he went along. He
was singing:

> I came home one summer night
> To find your heart fire burning bright,
> Baby, bring your love to me,
> I'll throw it all away-ay,
> I'll throw it all away.

> Husks of stars and diamond rings,
> And all alive and burning things,
> Bring them here to me, babe,
> I'll throw them all away-ay,
> I'll throw them all away.

Stu's Song

JANICE HARRELL

CROSSWINDS

New York • Toronto
Sydney • Auckland
Manila

First publication July 1988

ISBN 0-373-98028-0

Printed in the U.S.A.

RL 7.1, IL age 12 and up

JANICE HARRELL earned her M.A. and Ph.D. from the University of Florida, and for a number of years taught English at the college level. She is the author of a number of books for teens, as well as a mystery novel for adults. She lives in North Carolina.

Chapter One

If you could believe my parents, my best friend, Rudene, lived a life of constant danger. For one thing, her family lived in a trailer, and as Mama pointed out, a mobile-home unit could burn from stem to stern in five minutes flat. Nor was the trailer the only danger Mama saw. Rudene's family had a sizeable flock of chickens, all of them, according to Mama, molting both dirty feathers and dangerous salmonella germs. Worse, out back, her father was raising some calves. "I do wish you'd be careful when you go back there, Lang," Mama told me. "That shed is bound to be full of tetanus germs. One scratch with a nail and you'll have lockjaw before you know it."

My mother was the sort of person who actually read the accident and crime reports in the local newspaper every day, because she said she wanted to know what to watch out for. She liked Rudene's family, but she could not understand their point of view. "They aren't even saving for a house," she said. "I can tell they can't be by the way they keep buying VCRs and pickup trucks. And all those dogs, eating their heads off! How can they expect to save for a house that way?"

What Mama did not understand was that Rudene's family did not want a house. The old greenish-brown trailer, to which Rudene's dad had added a front porch, had been sitting in the same place for so long, growing gently more dilapidated every year, that it had begun to look soft and natural around the edges, as if it had grown up from the deeply rutted earth, and they liked it that way. Situated around it, helter-skelter, were the various dwellings of Rudene's aunts, uncles and cousins, some living in trailers and some living in small white houses made of asbestos shingle.

By most standards the place wasn't the prettiest, with all its muddy driveways. Tufts of crabgrass and dandelions eked out an existence only in the few patches where the family's pickup trucks didn't go. But it had a nice country feel to it. I always liked visiting out there, helping give the calves their bottles, checking out the newly hatched chicks or leafing through the snapshots of the latest Harper family wedding or christening.

The road Rudene lived on was called Harper's Road because nobody but Harpers lived on it. The Harpers were a prime example of what is meant by "having roots." When they furthered their education they did it at Siler Tech or Siler Falls Christian College, and afterward they invariably went to work somewhere around town. A Harper would no more have thought about going to Raleigh to look for a job than he would have thought about emigrating to Japan. With my own graduation and departure from home looming ahead of me, I couldn't help but envy them that.

This morning, I noticed that under a clutch of mailboxes labeled A. Harper, A. Harper, Jr., Billy Harper and Lamar Harper, Esq. the sun was dancing in the dew caught by some lacy weeds. Fluffy white clouds were floating over the trailers, and Harper's Road looked like a bite taken out of heaven.

I tapped my horn, and Rudene appeared at her door. She skipped down the cement-block steps of the porch, trying to smooth her hair with her hand. A big black dog moved, yawning, and rearranged himself in a different spot of sun. Rudene's family had a lot of dogs—spaniels for house pets, hounds and beagles for hunting and a couple of big, shaggy mongrels whose only mission in life, as far as I could tell, was to lie around in the sunshine and make the rest of us feel energetic by comparison. Watching Rudene, I decided that she was a little like a dog herself, a part-cocker puppy maybe. She was bouncy with wavy chestnut hair and an open, friendly face full of freckles that looked as if it had never known a secret, much less kept one.

She threw open the car door and scooted onto the passenger seat next to me. "Did you hear about the wild party at Flip Truman's?" she asked breathlessly. "Daddy heard about it at work. 'Course, nobody said a word about it to Mr. Truman. Daddy said this absolute dead silence would fall whenever Mr. Truman came around by the coffee urn. But as soon as he'd go, everybody'd start talking about it again. Daddy said there was twenty-five thousand dollars worth of damage to the inside of the house. Can you believe it?"

I could believe it.

"What everybody's saying is Flip's parents were out of town and he was supposed to be staying with Mickey Brumble, but it turned out he sneaked back to his house and threw this party. I was so surprised I just about dropped my teeth. I didn't know Flip was like that."

"Maybe he didn't plan for the party to be so wild," I suggested cautiously. "Maybe it got out of hand." I don't know why I didn't tell Rudene outright that I had been at the party. I guess I was still finding it a little hard to believe myself.

"Twenty-five thousand dollars worth of damage," she repeated. "They must have pretty well trashed the place."

I backed out of the muddy driveway carefully so as to avoid hitting any dogs. The one thing that could stir those mongrels into action was for you to start backing out onto the road. One or the other of them never failed to amble into the path of the car.

"Shoo," said Rudene, leaning out the open window. "Get on back, Blue."

When we got to school, we hadn't been out of the car two seconds before Lori Owens materialized at my left elbow and began babbling excitedly, "Were you there when the cops came, Lang? Tell me what happened! Larry and I left early. Larry says we should be glad, but what I say is we missed the whole thing. When we left the only thing that had happened was Melissa throwing up on the couch, and you can't call that exactly big excitement."

I hunched my shoulders and tried to disappear into the pavement. "I left early, too," I said, speeding up my steps to outdistance her.

"Okay, be that way!" she shouted at my back.

Rudene was trotting along beside me. "Why didn't you tell me you were at the party, Lang?" she asked mournfully. "I tell you everything. I told you what I made in trig. I told you all about my crush on Mike. I even told you when I flunked the driver's test. And here you're a genuine eyewitness at a party that rates practically as a major disaster and you don't even tell me."

"I wasn't exactly at the party," I said. "I mean, at least I did leave early just the way I said. When they started stacking up the living room furniture to see how high it would reach, I was out of there." I glanced swiftly around me to make sure nobody was listening. "As a matter of fact, I was the one who called the police. You know I don't go to wild parties. I just happened to go by there for a little while with Stu."

"Oh, you went with Stu," said Rudene, exhaling. "That explains it. Okay, so what made you call the police? What on earth was going on over there?"

"Actually, I'm not really sure of everything that happened. A mob of kids was there, and there was a lot of confusion. I don't know where they all came from, and I have no idea what they were all doing. They must have broken into the Trumans' liquor cabinet, though, because there were bottles all over the place. Some guys who were wrestling had fallen right into the stereo system. Of course, Stu loved it. You know Stu, he's sort of a connoisseur of chaos. So he sat down at the piano and started to sing. You know the way he sings.''

"Yeah," she sighed.

"He may have made the song up on the spot for all I know, but one thing was for sure—it was only one step away from inciting a riot. The refrain went something like 'burning burning, higher and higher.' You get the drift. It just whipped them up more. People started diving off the deck into the lake. I could hear them yelling and splashing out there. I think they were trying to have some sort of swimming race.''

"Okay, I get the stereo, the stacked furniture and the swimming in the lake," said Rudene. "But I still can't figure out how it adds up to twenty-five thousand dollars worth of damage.''

"I can tell you this much—when I left I saw people I didn't even know carrying things out to their cars— tape decks, televisions.''

"No! Didn't Flip try to stop them?''

"He was out," I said tersely.

"You mean he wasn't even at his own party?''

"No, I mean passed out. Out cold.''

"Golly!" said Rudene. To my relief the bell rang. I was not particularly concerned about the ruin of the Trumans' house, though, heaven knows, that was bad enough. I had my own reasons for preferring not to think about that night. I wanted to push the memory of it far back into the recesses of my mind. And it was going to be hard to do that with the party clearly destined to go down as one of the classic, all-time wild bashes of Siler Falls. People would be talking about it for months.

That afternoon I had to stay after school for an emergency meeting of the prom decoration committee that our chairman, Mitzi Summerall, had called. "It was a mistake," Mitzi cried. Her face was pink and her barrettes had gotten pulled askew where she had torn at her hair. She no longer looked like Mitzi Summerall, vice president of the student body, sweetheart of the Wheel Club and head cheerleader—she looked like a Cabbage Patch Kid left out in the rain. "We never should have picked Fantasia for a theme. It's going to be awful. People are going to say it's just plain dumb, that's what. I know it, I just know it. Tony Barnett already told me it sounded like we were making decorations for a gay bar."

"How would he know?" snickered Michael. Mitzi didn't even hear him.

"And now we can't even get the chicken wire. Everybody's saying they don't have chicken wire and they can't get chicken wire. It's some kind of shortage or something," she cried. "You know we can't do

Fantasia without chicken wire. We're going to have to change the theme."

Each and every one of us had spent hours slaving over the creation of two giant polka-dot mushrooms, mushrooms that were even now stored in Vern Prendergrass's garage, so Mitzi's defeatist attitude about the Fantasia theme won her no friends on the committee. If we changed the theme, what were we going to do with those two giant mushrooms?

"If you can't stand the heat, stay out of the kitchen," snarled Vern.

"I resign!" shrieked Mitzi. "If you think you're so smart, Vern Prendergrass, you go find the chicken wire."

I felt sorry for her. A lifetime of popularity is no preparation for being chairman of the prom decoration committee where any decision you make is bound to meet with schoolwide criticism if not outright ridicule. But I had no time to comfort Mitzi. From my point of view, the crucial thing was to be sure I didn't get stuck with her job myself. Vern was already casting his eye about the room for a likely replacement. As Mitzi sobbed her way out the door, I moved swiftly. "I nominate Suzy Harkness for chairman," I said. Suzy looked pleased, and I beamed at her. The very last thing I wanted was to spend the final golden hours of my senior year worrying about chicken wire.

By the time I got home, I was wilted. Instead of calling out my usual hello, I slunk past the kitchen toward my room. Even my hair was limp.

As I passed I heard Dad's voice in the kitchen. It was odd for him to be home in the afternoon, and I wondered what was going on. The kitchen door was closed but I could hear scraps of what he was saying and the occasional murmur of Mama's voice.

I heard him say, "fractured cranium, crushed cervical vertebrae...nothing..." My father is an ear, nose and throat specialist and spends most of his professional life dealing with people's sinus trouble, so I couldn't see, at first, what he was talking about. He must have come upon the scene of an accident, I figured.

I pushed the kitchen door open, and my parents' white faces slowly turned toward me. "What's wrong?" I cried.

"Stu crashed his motorcycle," said Mama.

"Is he hurt? Is he in the hospital?"

"Lang," said my father softly, "he's gone."

I sat down suddenly in the kitchen chair, feeling a kind of blankness close over me for a minute. I was dimly aware of Mama kneeling beside me, putting her arm around me. She was crying.

"I can't believe it," I said. "I just saw him. He was just here. I just saw him Saturday night." It was frightening the way the bottom seemed to be falling out of my stomach. My head seemed too hot and swollen. I jumped up and ran to my room.

A minute later I heard a tapping on my door. "Lang?" my mother called gently. "Langdon, honey, can I get you anything?"

"I'm okay," I said. Actually, pain gripped my whole body. I wondered if it were going to kill me.

"Okay, honey. You come in the kitchen if you want to talk some more," she said.

"Mama?" I called.

She opened the door and came in.

"Did Dad see it?"

"He came by right afterward. There wasn't anything anybody could have done, sweetheart. It must have been instantaneous."

"Where? Where did it happen?"

"The intersection of Thirteenth and Vine."

She gave me a pitying look.

"I'll be fine," I said. "I'll be fine. You go on."

She closed the door behind her. I wondered if, when they gave you a sedative, you came out of it and started feeling this way over again, as if it had just happened. I would have liked to go to sleep for three days and wake up when I was over the shock.

And yet the odd thing was that though I was sitting there quivering, I wasn't surprised. Mama had said all along that Stu would kill himself on that motorcycle. And now he had gone and done it. The motorcycle wreck felt like the continuation of a quarrel between the two of us, as if he had wrecked his cycle to get back at me. I could almost hear him saying, "Bet *you* can't do that."

Wednesday afternoon, Mama and Dad and I went to the funeral. It was hard for me to remember that only days before I had been deep into the politics of prom decorations. School seemed far away, like another life that I only dimly remembered.

It was a cold day for March, and the sun, sinking lower in the sky, was casting unnaturally sharp, long shadows. The black iron fence that encircled the churchyard threw a wavy shadow on the scraggly grass. Even the pebbles embedded in the cement walkway cast small shadows like crooked pennies. I watched with fascination as my own shadow preceded me up the church walkway, and I tried to remember if things had ever looked exactly this way to me before.

Behind another handful of mourners we filed into the church. With Mama and Dad, I stood in the aisle for a second waiting for my eyes to adjust to the dim light. The church was filled with people sitting silently in pews, dressed in their best clothes. Doleful, soupy sounds poured out of the organ. The coffin stood in front of the communion rail, covered with a florist's blanket of greenery.

The collar of my blouse was tight around my neck, and I wondered if I would be able to get to our pew and unbutton it before I choked.

Mama and Dad and I took a pew midway, next to a stained-glass window of Jesus holding a lamb and a shepherd's crook. When we were walking up the aisle there had been moments when it had seemed none of this could be happening, that we were the victims of some practical joke. But by the time I sat down and began fumbling with the first button of my blouse, I was thinking it was the most real thing that had ever happened to me.

A moment later the dark wood of the pew in front of me lightened a little, and I knew the church door had opened. I looked back and saw Stu's family coming in. Mrs. Saranin's eyes were glazed and it was only with her husband's help that she was able to totter up the aisle. As Dr. and Mrs. Saranin passed by our pew, I saw that Elinor and Brian were behind them, their eyes swollen and their damp lashes sticking together in starry points. Next came Stu's grandmother, old Mrs. Saranin, tiny, yellow-skinned and incredibly wrinkled, leaning on the arm of Stu's Uncle Adam. A young blond woman I didn't know was on the other side of his grandmother. She reminded me of someone, but I couldn't think who. She was too blond to be a Saranin but was wearing a navy blue suit with white piping that made me wonder if she had gone shopping for it with Stu's mother. It was exactly the sort of outfit Mrs. S. liked, something that would have been perfect for a Junior League meeting twenty years ago.

"That's his fiancée," someone whispered behind me as the family moved out of earshot.

My hymnal slipped out of my fingers, and I bent over suddenly, glad to kneel down below the level of the pews where I could hide my face and have some excuse for the blood rushing to it.

I straightened up carefully, holding my hymnal very tightly so that the skin around my nails turned pale and milky, as if I were hemorrhaging internally. I had suddenly realized who the girl reminded me of. She reminded me of myself. She was slender, like me, and with the cool blond look I recognized as my own. Was it possible that she *was* me? That I was gliding up the aisle with Stu's family and that it was some other girl sitting in the pew thinking that her panty hose were too tight and that her blouse was choking her?

The organ began playing "Rock of Ages." The notes dragged along as if they were being pulled uphill by their noses. I supposed the Saranins had requested that piece especially. It was the sort of dour, respectable thing they might have liked. It was as if at Stu's funeral they were trying to make him out to be the conventional person he would never agree to be back when he had the strength to have any say in the matter.

I was having trouble thinking of Stu as dead. It was easier to imagine that he just wasn't around much anymore, the way it had been in the fall when he went off to college. This won't be so different, I told myself. He hasn't been around much lately. Now he'll be around even less, that's all.

After the service, when we came out of the church into the bright sunshine, I almost lost my footing on the stairs, and Dad had to steady me by holding on to my elbow. I squinted at the sun, hanging lower now in the sky, then turned to Dad. "Let's skip the graveside service, okay?" I said.

"Well, I don't know," said Mama. "Poor Mary will expect—"

"We're skipping it, Sara," said Dad, guiding me toward our parked car. "Lang's had enough."

Mama hurried along behind us, her high heels clicking on the pavement. Dad would take care of me. I wouldn't have to go now to watch them lower that coffin into the ground. Maybe I would live through this, after all.

The funny thing was that after the funeral life went on as usual, which would have surprised Stu. He concentrated so much on himself that he expected every-one else to, too. A couple of the guys Stu knew at college, Bob Deans and Phil Dixon, left directly after the funeral and drove straight down to Fort Lauder-dale for the rest of their spring break. They got ar-rested the second day they were down there and had to phone home for bail. I ran into Phil in front of the frozen pizzas at Safeway the day he got back. He was pretty mad that he had gotten arrested before he even got a tan.

"I've had better vacations," he said. He was hold-ing a large frozen pizza in his hands, squinting at its label. Behind him white clouds of cold air were escap-ing from the glass freezer door he had left open. "Hey, have you tried this pizza with the mushrooms and pepperoni added? Is it any good?" I told him that I couldn't recommend it.

At school, the prom decoration committee was re-covering from Mitzi's defection. Our new chairman, Suzy, had found a seed supply store in Wilson that promised us up to seven hundred yards of chicken wire, which sounded like plenty. All we needed to do now was to construct a tunnel of love covered with tissue paper flowers and then have enough chicken wire left for three giant pink butterflies.

The day after Suzy got the chicken-wire order pinned down, I was walking down A wing's hall when

I heard somebody say, "And if I know Stu, he was drunk out of his mind when it happened." I had to close my eyes and catch my breath, the pain in my chest caught me so much by surprise. I understood then why widows used to wear black back in Victorian times. It was so people would watch what they said around them. I was dressed in jeans and a sweatshirt depicting four hippos in a tug-of-war with a yellow butterfly, so everybody felt free to make cracks about Stu. I was afraid for a minute that I might pass out.

"It's the surprise," I explained afterward to Rudene, when we were eating lunch. "I mean, it happened. There it is, right? I'm used to it. It's not that I mind people talking about it. I just don't want to be caught by surprise, that's all."

"Chris saw it happen," Rudene said in a dreamy voice.

"Chris?"

"My cousin Chris."

"I didn't know you had a cousin named Chris," I said irritably. I wasn't sure I could have named every one of Rudene's cousins, but I could have sworn none of them had names like Chris. They were all called things like Tommy or Billy or Wesley, good solid country names of the sort you might meet with on any back road in North Carolina.

"He's been living out in California," said Rudene. She began manipulating a squishy pat of butter off its little square of paper, trying to get it onto her soft roll. "Before that he lived in Texas, and before that I think he was in Georgia. They've moved around a lot. His dad is in the service. Like I was saying, Chris was coming down Thirteenth Street when he heard the crash. That was when the bike hit the truck, you see. The next thing he knew he saw this body lying there on the sidewalk and all these cars were stopping and people jumping out and running over to the guy on the sidewalk, so then he left. He told me the cycle was on fire. Stu's cycle, I mean. It was lying there already black as charcoal, and it was still burning. Of course, Chris didn't know then that it was Stu's cycle."

"That was helpful of him, just driving on as if nothing had happened."

"He didn't want to add to all the mess. You know how people stand around and gawk after an accident. Look, I thought you said you didn't care if people talked about it."

"That doesn't mean I want to go over every grisly detail. That's being morbid. What I meant was I don't mind if people talk about it in a general way. As long as it doesn't take me by surprise, that is. You know what I mean."

"Yep. You mean you don't want to talk about it. I'm sorry I said anything. Forget it, honestly. Don't you think you'd better put your head down between your knees? You look awful. Are you going to faint?"

"I am fine. I am not going to faint. I never faint. I'm not the kind of person who faints."

"Maybe you'd better put your head down a minute just in case," said Rudene.

Late that afternoon, after I got in from school and took the evening paper out of the mailbox, I saw that the skies were low and dark. On page two the paper was prophesying rain and snow flurries. "Well," said Mama, as she lifted a big pot of geraniums and pressed it firmly against her midriff, "this time March came in like a lamb and is going out like a lion."

I put the paper down on the deck and helped her carry the geraniums and begonias inside to a safe refuge in the atrium. We nestled the pots in between the ferns and tropical plants. My grandfather, the architect, had designed our house. That was why we were the only people in Siler Falls with an atrium, which is like a doughnut hole in the middle of the house. Except for a screen over its top, our atrium was open to the sky, like any other garden. A drain had been cut in its stone paved floor so the rain water could run out.

Looking at our house, I think I might have guessed that it had been built for an inward-looking, private

kind of family, because an atrium is, as I see it, a way
of having a private out-of-doors. Some people might
consider having a private out-of-doors a slightly ex-
treme step, but my parents loved the idea. Dad had
installed a sunken hot tub between the ficus tree and
the philodendron. He said it was not a luxury but
therapeutic because it was a lot better to go out there
and soak than to drink a martini.

The tub hadn't been used at all the week after Stu's
funeral. What with Dad's moving his appointments
around to make room for the funeral and with his
trying to spend some time with Dr. Saranin, who was
wild with grief, he had been getting in even later than
usual and hadn't had time for any of his usual soak-
ing. I noticed a couple of crisp brown ficus leaves lying
on the hot tub's cover. The air in the atrium felt damp
and close to my face.

Mama put down the last pot of begonias and
looked up at me with concern. "Why don't you go lie
down, Lang? I'll bring you some hot chocolate. You
look so peaked." She put her hand on my forehead.
"No fever, anyway. Are you taking your vitamins?"

"I'm tired," I said. "After I do my physics, maybe
I'll go on to bed."

"That's a good idea. I expect a rest is what you
need," she said.

After I finished my homework, I fixed myself a grilled cheese sandwich and ate a few orange sections. Then I went into my room and put on my nightgown. As I slipped in between the sheets, I could hear drops of rain hitting hard against the windows. It sounded as if rice were being thrown against the glass. Outside, wind was whistling in the pines. Our house was set back a little from the street in a pine woods, and the lot was so large that the house had a lonely feel to it even though it was in a neighborhood. I was glad my bedroom faced the street because that meant I could look out my window at night and see the neighbor's lights. It made me feel a little less as if I were the last person awake in the whole world.

I snuggled down under the comforter, listening to the wind and yearning for spring to make up its mind to come to stay. I hated the kind of weather that rattled the trees, blew the daffodils flat down against the dirt and made you feel somehow that things were coming unstuck.

Suddenly I heard a sharp crack against my window. I sat up and looked out the window, my heart squeezing painfully inside me. But no one was down on the lawn. It had only been a falling pine cone that hit my window. Not Stu.

Chapter Two

In the ninth grade Stu had been plump. Not fat exactly, but a boy who couldn't pass up a Whopper or a peanut butter and jelly sandwich with a double-chocolate malted milk to save his life. His hair was thick and dark and curled a little at the back of his neck. It was not all that long—nobody else would have thought twice about it—but he had a never-ending battle with his dad over it. Dr. Saranin wanted Stu's hair cut so short no one would ever have known about the girlish curl that was hiding in it aching to express itself. Naturally, Stu fought his father every inch of the way. One time, Mrs. Saranin locked Stu out of the

house and said he couldn't come in until he got a
haircut because those curls were about to give his father a heart attack. I couldn't understand what the
commotion was about. I loved Stu's hair. Those few
loose, soft half curls at the base of his neck were the
kind of curls that wrapped themselves right around
your heart and wouldn't let you go. Of course, that
may have been what Dr. Saranin didn't like about
them.

The night before my thirteenth birthday I woke up
suddenly just after midnight. Later I realized that it
must have been the sound of a rock hitting against my
window that woke me, but at the time I was scared. I
jumped up, clutching my bedspread to my chest, and
peeked out the front window. Below, on the close-cut
grass, I could make out a figure in a white shirt. I
cracked the window a little and stared down as if my
eyes were strung on a piece of fishing line that ran
right down to the boy standing on the grass.

"Lang!" he yelled. "Come on down."

"Stu! What are you doing over here? It's the middle of the night!"

"Come on down and I'll tell you."

I was afraid my parents were going to hear him
yelling, so I quickly went out the back door and onto
the deck. I made my way down the long stairway from
the deck to the lawn that had been cleared among the

pines. It made me feel almost light-headed to be outside in my nightgown with the moon shining on the white azaleas—as if I had rashly drunk or eaten one of those mysterious morsels Alice was always coming upon in Wonderland and was waiting to see what was going to happen to me next. It seemed as if I might easily grow to some incredible height or shrink as small as a beetle. The grass was cold under my bare feet and as full of air as a pillow. Over in front of the azaleas Stu was waiting for me, his white shirt catching the moonlight and making him a pale silhouette against the dark pines. He came closer so that I could make out his face and said, "Happy birthday. Sit down."

I sat down on the wet grass in my nightgown. Stu had that kind of effect on me. I was like a person hypnotized. I didn't even say, "Where?" I just folded up like a paper fan and sat.

He lifted a paperback and began to read in a low voice, "'My birthday began with the water/Birds and the birds of the winged trees flying my name.'"

I couldn't believe that Stu had actually come over and waked me up in the middle of the night to read me *Fern Hill*! I was charmed. I knew he was out-of-his-mind crazy, but it was as if his very craziness cast a spell on me, and I found myself looking up at his pale face as if I were trying to memorize it. Or maybe it wasn't a spell but something inside of me that drew me to Stu. I don't know.

After that night he got in the habit of walking with me to school. That was back before they built the new high school. That year and the next the ninth graders had to go to the junior high, which was within walking distance of our houses. Elinor and Brian, Stu's brother and sister, walked with us part of the way until they got to Nottingham Lane, where they turned off to go to Fox Hill Elementary. Stu was supposed to be keeping an eye on them, but half the time he teased them until they cried and the other half he ignored them.

It was funny to see how Brian blushed with pleasure when Stu bothered to treat him with basic human decency. He worshiped Stu. My theory was that Stu was nice to his brother and sister at home and was only mean to them when other people were around. But maybe I was wrong about that. Maybe Stu was mean all the time but Brian worshiped him anyway. Maybe Brian couldn't help himself any more than I could help the way I felt. Stu was so special, so clever, you couldn't help looking up to him.

I wrote "Lang and Stu" in ballpoint pen on my notebook. I wasn't perfectly happy with the way it looked because the blue letters ran along the threads of the fabric cover and our names came out blocky and square. That didn't suit my ideas, which ran more to swirls and flourishes and heart-shaped letters, but I told myself the sentiment was the important thing.

The next morning, when Stu saw the notebook, he hooted. "Lang and Stu," he sneered.

At first I couldn't make out what I had done wrong. He had treated me to an ice-cream sundae, hadn't he? He had asked me to the ninth grade sock hop. He brought over his private notebooks of sketches and poetry to show me. Wasn't I entitled to write "Lang and Stu"?

"What's wrong with it?" I asked, flushing.

"It's so hokey," he said. "You want a friendship ring, next, Lang? You want to wear matching T-shirts? His and hers T-shirts?"

Both the friendship ring and the matching T-shirts sounded good to me, but I sensed these gestures of belonging were second-rate somehow in Stu's eyes, and I felt ashamed.

When I got home from school, I went out on the back deck to the barbecue grill. Piling the briquettes into a pyramid the way the package directions said, I doused them with lighter fluid and touched a match to them. When the coals were gray and powdery on the outside, I began broiling my notebook.

"Do I smell lighter fluid?" said Mama. She had come out on the deck. My mother could smell danger from miles away. "Something's burning! Langdon, what on earth are you doing?"

"Burning my notebook."

"The smell is terrible. I wouldn't be a bit surprised if that material is toxic when burned. Here, honey," she said, grabbing me by the shoulders, "stand upwind of it. Why would you burn your notebook? Why can't you just throw things away like everyone else? Goodness gracious, look at that ash. It will be getting all over the place. Honestly, Langdon Emily Devereaux, you act as if you've taken leave of your senses, burning notebooks. What next?"

I looked at the smoldering notebook almost with puzzlement. I had burned it because I didn't want even the garbage collectors to see it. Above all, I was afraid the notebook might tumble out of the trash can as it was carried to the truck. Then Stu might find it and laugh at it again. But Mama was right, I thought. It was crazy. This wasn't the kind of thing I would do. It was the kind of thing Stu would do. I could almost hear him announcing, "'Pavane for a Dead Notebook,'" and strumming some mock-gruesome tune on the piano.

"Next time I'll just throw it away," I said.

"Good," said Mama, ushering me inside. "And next time, Lang, please check with me before you light a fire. Fires can be very dangerous. Why, do you realize those cans of lighter fluid can actually explode?''

I felt a little rush of tenderness toward her, thinking of how hard she worked night and day to keep harm from me. Now that Stu had come into my life, I could understand all her worry better, somehow. I had the feeling that Stu should be marked with a sign that said Danger—Keep Away.

The next day I went by the drugstore and bought a new plastic-covered red notebook that folded over and snapped on the side. It had five dividers and three pockets inside, plus a pencil sharpener, a ruler and a protractor. All in all it was an impressive notebook, one nobody could laugh at.

''Langdon and Stu, sitting in a tree, k-i-s-s-i-n-g,'' chanted Elinor and Brian behind us. I thought they had picked up their devilish tricks from Stu. It stood to reason that if kids were teased they learned to tease back. On the other hand, maybe kids would tease no matter what. Maybe that's what's meant by original sin.

Stu turned on them, snarling. ''Go home,'' he said. In one quick step he was upon Brian and twisting his arm behind his back.

Brian screamed, ''You're hurting me!''

''Go home,'' Stu said between clenched teeth. ''Do you hear me?''

Elinor and I watched, our faces tight with anxiety. Stu never laid a hand on Elinor, rightly figuring that just seeing what he did to Brian was enough to keep her in line. I had read it could be more frightening to watch violence than to have it actually happen to you. Judging from my own experience, I think that might be true.

Stu flung Brian to the grass, where he sat sniffling. "Now don't give me any more trouble, do you hear?" said Stu. "Go on home. I didn't mean to hurt you."

I guess Brian believed that. I didn't. And I thought Stu was too old to be beating up on his younger brother. But I reminded myself that being an only child I didn't really understand the way brothers and sisters got along.

Mama was off at a meeting of the medical auxiliary, but that didn't matter. Stu, living right down the street and being Dr. Saranin's son, was in and out of our house all the time. We went on in and got some lemonade and potato chips from the kitchen. My room, in keeping with my family's respect for privacy, was almost a self-contained apartment. The bedroom had not just an adjoining bathroom, but a separate sitting room that doubled as a study.

I put the bowl of potato chips on the coffee table there, and sat down on the couch to watch Stu pace the floor. He was in the tenth grade now, and I was in the ninth. He was taking geometry, had a learner's permit and was allowed to stay up past midnight. I had the gnawing feeling that he would always be just one step ahead of me.

He pulled a book off the shelves. *"The Rubáiyát of Omar Khayyám,"* he said, saying the syllables slowly to savor them. He flipped it open. "Have you read it yet?"

"Sure," I said. I read all the books Stu recommended to me. I read a lot, anyway. I was one of those people who, if it came to choosing between reading and eating, would be hard pressed to make a decision. Stu, though, had lately come to look as if he had made the decision in favor of books. He read everything in sight, including lots of weird books he had to get on interlibrary loan. Mrs. Elkins said she loved to see Stu heading back to the reference desk because he always presented her with a real challenge.

On the other hand, he had practically given up eating and had lost so much weight that for the first time I could see the bony structure of his face. His cheekbones were so well-defined that you could follow the curve of them from below his eyes almost to his mouth, and his chin, slightly cleft, was stern. It made me anxious because he had gotten good-looking and I was still wearing braces. He had hips as slender as a toreador's, and his jeans were so tight it was embarrassing. He was not handsome in a football player kind of way, but he had a dark kind of good looks that seemed almost a taunt in the face of ordinary ideas of handsomeness. I was afraid one of the beautiful older girls at the high school would steal him away.

Stu put the book down and went over to look out the window. "Pick a book, any book," he said.

At first I was surprised he was talking to me. It had sounded as if maybe he were starting a conversation with a pine tree. "You mean, pick a book off the shelf?"

"That's right. I won't look. Pick any book and read me a paragraph out of it. I'll tell you who wrote it."

"Is this going to be like a card trick?"

"Do you have to keep asking questions, Lang? Who are you, Sam Donaldson? Pick a book."

I walked over to the shelf and pulled out a book Stu had given me. I read, "'But when I myself got to know the Natives, this quality in them was one of the things I liked best. They had real courage: the unadulterated liking of danger.'"

"Isak Dinesen, *Out of Africa*," he said at once. "I gave you that one. Pick something tougher."

Irritated by his confidence, I chose a nondescript passage out of *David Copperfield*, a favorite book of mine but not at all Stu's kind of thing. "Dickens," he said offhandedly. The game went on through ten more books, and I wasn't able to stump him. He had an almost-photographic memory and an uncanny ear for an author's style of expression.

He turned around to face me, looking pleased. "Bet you can't do that," he said.

"One more," I said.

When he had turned away, I stealthily plucked *Little Women* from the shelf. Flipping through it, I chose as bland a passage as I could quickly find.

After I read it to him, he stood very still, and I knew at once that I had him. There was a moment's silence, and then he said, "You didn't make that one up, did you?"

"Nope."

He wheeled around, and I gleefully held the book up for his inspection.

"*Little Women?*" he said. "You've got to be kidding. *Little Women*?"

"It's a book."

"But Louisa May Alcott? The woman's obscene— Marmie and all the good little girls."

"It's a good book," I said. "Have you read it?"

He took it out of my hands and, his lips set grimly, headed out the door.

"Where are you going?"

"I'm going to go read *Little Women*."

Reading *Little Women* must have been a penance to Stu. He did not like stories about ordinary people. What he liked was to get hold of some author who thought he was better than everybody else, some writer who spent his spare time wasting money, drinking himself to death, killing big-game animals, or kicking peasants around. Good citizenship didn't interest Stu. He liked pointless danger and weird psychic experiences. Offhand I couldn't think of anyone whose tastes differed more strikingly from my own.

I suppose there were people who thought our friendship was strange.

Chapter Three

It took a while for it to dawn on me that the reason Stu's family had quit harassing him about his hair was that by the time he got to be sixteen they had bigger things to worry about.

"Can I spend the night, Mrs. Devereaux?" asked Stu one afternoon.

"Why, Stu, is anything wrong?"

"Troubles at home," he said sadly.

I could sense Mama's panic as she dealt with an internal battle between her desire to help, her respect for people's privacy and her respect for the conventions. Pins under her fingernails wouldn't have forced her to ask Stu what *kind* of trouble at home, though I was sure she feared the worst—alcoholism, spouse abuse, chains in the basement. But whatever was going on over at the Saranins', she still felt uncomfortable getting between Stu and his parents. "Well," she said weakly, "if it's all right with your parents. Why don't you call them?"

"Or I could sleep down at that shelter at the church."

Mama shuddered at the thought of Stu bedding down on the cement floor of the church basement with the city's derelicts. She caved in at once. "No, of course, Stu, you can stay here. We've got plenty of room."

I wasn't surprised later that night to hear Stu's fingernails tapping at my bedroom door. I pulled the covers up to my chin, rolled over to face the door and said, "Come on in, Stu. It's not locked." I reached back to switch on the night-light at the head of my bed.

I had never thought before what funny pajamas my father wore until I saw Stu in them. They were baggy, tied at the waist with a drawstring and decorated with red, white and blue clocks. Stu was wearing only the bottoms, and his slender waist and sleek chest rose out of the slapstick bagginess of the pajama bottoms with the incongruity of some carved pagan idol dressed in a missionary's bloomers.

"It's cold in here," he said. "Brrr."

"Fresh air is good for you," I said. "You can put on my bathrobe if you're cold. It's right there on the back of the door."

"I can't just get under the covers with you?" he asked.

"What's really going on with your family, Stu? Did they lock you out the way you told Mama?"

"Do I lie? Sure, they locked me out. It's the grades thing again. Dad chased me through the den with a tennis racket this morning. I had a bad minute there when I thought he had me cornered, but I just ducked under his left arm and took off. His reflexes are in sad shape. Lucky thing."

"Wouldn't it be easier just to bring up your grades?"

"Hey, whose life is this, anyway? And whose side are you on?"

"But if you don't bring up your grades, you'll never get into a decent college."

"Stop right there, Lang. You're sounding just like my father."

I fell silent. I knew that in Stu's book there was nothing worse than sounding like his father.

He pulled a chair over next to the bed and straddled it. "Have you ever heard of Cronus?"

"The Titan," I said. I was proud of nailing down the reference. "He was the father of Zeus."

"Cronus ate his children," said Stu. "He was afraid one of his children was going to grow up and supplant him, so he ate them. That's my father—Cronus. He wants to devour me, digest me and completely assimilate my body so that it becomes a part of him. I would look like him, talk like him, think like him, go to a good college and vote Republican just the way he does. Do you understand what I'm saying? I'm not going to let him do that to me."

He reached out and flipped back my covers. I scrambled to pull them up again.

"Come on Lang," he said. "Let's get warm together."

I think my voice must have showed how shaken I was. "You'd better get back to your room, Stu, or my father's going to be the one chasing you with a tennis racket."

He stood up. "Okay," he said. "I'm going. See? You always play it safe, don't you?"

"Oh, I don't know. If I'm friends with you I can't be all *that* careful."

"That's only because I have the adventures you'd like to have. I remind you that you're alive, while you just sit around the house here, being careful all the time.''

"Couldn't it be that I like you? Couldn't it be something obvious like that? Does the reason for something always have to sound like something out of a book?''

The door closed quietly. Stu was so melodramatic, I thought irritably. And he definitely had a habit of ruining my night's sleep.

I knew Stu was having troubles at home, but he didn't talk about it much. Often I would hear a rock bang against my window in the middle of the night and go down to the lawn and listen to the strum of his guitar. He would sit cross-legged on the grass and sing very softly. He could almost have been singing to himself. But it wasn't always singing. He liked to talk to me about books he was reading, too. Other times he would tell me his endless dreamlike fantasies, as if he were some stoned Scheherazade.

He never slept very well, which probably explained why I saw so much of him at night. He once told me that when he was younger he would wake in the middle of the night and wander through the house opening bedroom doors, feeling frightened by the sight of sleeping bodies sprawled awkwardly on beds and by the strange light that spilled into the house from the streetlight. I think that panicky feeling in the middle of the night never left him. And when he got older it sent him over to my house where, desperate for company, he would throw a rock at my window and call me down.

Sometimes I felt as if Stu were my boyfriend. Other times that wasn't so clear. But I certainly thought that I understood him. I thought we were close. That much anyway.

It wasn't until I got my own driver's license that I discovered there was a part of his life I didn't even know about.

I was driving away from the post office, nervous about my first solo performance in the car. I was going very slowly, trying hard not to bump into any of the cars that were crowding around me. An impatient horn sounded behind me, and suddenly a car cut in ahead of me, narrowly missing an oncoming Cadillac. I could feel myself blushing. I hoped that when I got used to driving, I would remember some people out there might be beginners who had to go carefully just at first. Unconsciously, I slowed even more, and another horn sounded behind me. I felt like turning off the car and throwing my keys down on the street. If people insisted on blowing horns at me and getting me rattled, I could try blocking traffic completely and see how they liked that.

Suddenly, I saw that I was already at Hill Street, the street I was supposed to be turning onto. An oncoming pickup truck bore down on me with a roar, and I knew I wasn't up to finding a hole in the traffic and bolting through it. I had lost my nerve. There was no way I was going to be able to turn left.

Gritting my teeth, I kept driving. There had to be a traffic light somewhere, I told myself. Or at least a place farther on where the traffic wasn't so heavy.

I hadn't gone six blocks before I spotted Boomer Hill dead ahead. I turned the steering wheel sharply to the left. An oncoming Pontiac blared its horn. Flushing hotly, I refused to look in its direction as I turned onto Thomas, the major east-west artery bordering the Boomer Hill section. The good thing about driving, I saw now, was that you could step on the accelerator and leave your mistakes behind you. All those people who had decided I was an idiot back on Franklin Street were a quarter of a mile behind me. And I had turned just in time to escape driving into Boomer Hill. I was as relieved as if I had outswum a school of sharks.

The Boomer Hill section was within the city limits, but even though I had lived in Siler Falls my whole life, I had never ridden through it. It was a decayed section of the downtown area where drug busts were a way of life and where the major industries seemed to be burglary and homicide. Even respectable Thomas Street took on a sleazy air where it bordered the Hill. My car was now going past a pawn shop, an old movie theater with a crudely painted sign that said Temple of the Sacred Star, a shop that said OK Used Clothing and a couple of places where the windows had been boarded over.

Just then the light turned red, and I had to slow to a stop. Glancing around me I saw that I was beside a pool hall that stood on the corner of Thomas and Fenner at the eastmost point of Boomer Hill.

Leaning against the brick wall of the pool hall and sort of setting the tone of the place was a man wearing dusty black slacks and a sleeveless T-shirt that showed muscular arms covered with a web of blue tattoos. A cigarette dangled from his lower lip, and a thin plume of smoke floated above a pink, star-shaped scar on his cheek. Removing the cigarette, he yelled something to someone I couldn't see, and I noticed that one of his front teeth was capped with gold. I quickly checked to make sure my doors were all locked and reminded myself that a red light only lasted about three minutes.

A clamor of bells rang out imperiously and straight ahead of me I saw the railroad crossing bars slowly lowering. Siler Falls was the only town I had ever heard of that had a railroad running smack through the center of downtown, where it would cause the maximum inconvenience. Now I would have to wait until the train passed. I chewed uneasily on my thumbnail, reminding myself that the man in the T-shirt was most probably quite peaceable, just one of your basic, unemployed pool players, nothing frightening about him. At least he was carrying no visible weapons. I glanced around the car again to reassure myself that my doors were locked.

Ahead of me a whistle shrieked, and with a windy roar, the train began whizzing by. As far as I could see, it was a train that had no end. Its gleaming silver tail seemed to stretch to the horizon. I was stuck, all right. A line of cars had grown long behind me so I couldn't even back up. Not that I would have dreamed of backing up unless the man in the T-shirt had actually picked up a broken bottle and attacked my car. I was doing my best to appear cool. I began humming the theme song of *Mr. Rogers' Neighborhood*. I wished I were in that neighborhood instead of on the corner of Fenner and Thomas.

Meanwhile, I tried to keep an eye on the pool hall without being obvious about it. The big glass windows that fronted on the street were dusty, and some faded red letters over the open door said simply, B & K's Billiards. While I watched, a bunch of young black men tumbled out the front door onto the street as precipitously as if they had bounced off of a trampoline. I saw the flash of their teeth and got an impression of broad shoulders, tightly capped black hair and Banlon shirts that hugged their chests. They were laughing and holding beer cans. I decided they did not look like reliable taxpayers.

"Come on, come on, dumb train," I muttered, glancing anxiously at them. Then Stu stepped out of the pool hall. I watched, my mouth falling open in amazement, as he lazily leaned the dark curls of his head against the big store window. He was watching one of the young men toss a beer can at another. Foam brimmed out of the can all over the other guy's shirt, which made him choke with laughter. He threw the can down and kicked it, spilling beer out all over the sidewalk. All the other guys seemed to be doubling over, laughing themselves silly. I saw someone call to Stu and watched his lips move as he answered, but though I strained to hear I couldn't make out what he was saying over the roar of the train. I wished now that I had left my windows rolled down. I was so close I could have hit him with a spitball, but he didn't once look in my direction.

When a horn sounded behind me, at first I couldn't remember where I was. Then I saw that the train had gone. The light was green. Mechanically, I stepped on the accelerator and bumped my car across the tracks.

When I had crossed Main Street, I began breathing deeply for the first time in a quarter of an hour, but I felt sick. What was Stu doing at B & K's pool hall?

I knew I couldn't tell Mama about what I had seen. She might feel she had to inform Stu's parents, and if Stu ever found out I ratted on him, he would kill me. Or never speak to me again, which would be almost worse.

That night, as soon as we finished dinner at home, I drove over to Rudene's. I needed to talk about the thoughts that were buzzing around in my mind to the point that I couldn't sit still. I just wanted to make sense out of what I had seen so I could calm down and think about something else.

Rudene and I sat on her bed, the ribbed bedspread making furrows on my legs. "What can he be doing in that neighborhood?" I asked. "He looked as if he were part of that crowd. Why would Stu want to hang out at that pool hall?"

"Why don't you ask him?" she said. "Maybe he just likes to play pool."

I found it was hard to get across to Rudene the unsettling feeling I was having that I had discovered something Stu had meant to hide. It was as if he had a secret life.

"Have you ever been over on Boomer Hill?" I asked.

"Why would I go over there? Just a lot of condemned houses and bars and skinny dogs."

"Have you ever known *anybody* who spent any time over on Boomer Hill?"

"My cousin Billy used to take a shortcut right through there. I rode with him one time over to the junkyard where he goes to get parts for that old Ford of his. But his mama made him stop. Every time he'd stop at a red light, girls would come up to the car and proposition him. He thought it was kind of funny, but when Aunt Ruby found out about it, she made him start taking the long way around."

"Well, do you see what I mean? Everybody I know drives around the place. For one thing, it just isn't safe, all the awful things you hear about. *Nobody* goes over to Boomer Hill. What was Stu doing there?"

Rudene shrugged.

The next day I was out front getting the mail when Stu came roaring up on a motorcycle. The noise the thing made was so loud it seemed to vibrate in my bones. He was wearing black leather pants, black gloves and goggles. Astride the huge cycle he looked ominous enough to have been cast as one of the pursuing Fates in a Greek drama done in modern dress. With a mechanical cough, the bike choked down and he climbed off it and slipped the goggles off over his untidy hair.

"What do you think of her?"

"Big," I observed. The thing had silver exhaust pipes the size of my arm. "When did you get it?"

"Yesterday. I've been working nights and weekends, and I finally got enough to pay for her."

"I didn't know you'd been working," I said.

"Yeah."

"At a pool hall?"

He stared at me, then turned to dust an imaginary speck off the seat of the motorcycle. "I've been playing the piano at Fribble's six to nine. Good pay and good tips."

"The reason I thought maybe you were working at a pool hall is I happened to see you over at the pool hall on Fenner Street."

He turned and smiled at me. I could tell he had gotten over the jolt he felt on finding out that I knew about his other life and had begun enjoying himself. I wasn't sure I was altogether glad about that.

I sat down on the curb, my skirt spreading around me, and hugged my knees. "Do you go over to Boomer Hill much?"

"Yeah, I do. I like it over there. Neat people."

I found myself wondering if Stu was running drugs. I was surprised that I could even be thinking such a thing, but I knew I no longer had any idea what was going on with him.

"I thought it was mostly criminals that lived over there," I said.

"You've got it wrong," he said. "All kinds of people live there. Babies, dogs, numbers runners, druggies, people running little grocery stores, little old ladies, musicians down on their luck. The thing I like about it is everything's out in the open. People live in the streets, they fight, play ball, gamble and make love right out on the streets." He looked wordlessly around our street as if condemning in his mind the decorous blank-faced houses, barely visible on their large wooded lots. "Hop on the back of the bike, and I'll take you over there now. Come on, I'll show you some real life, Lang."

"I can't," I said. "I've got a date."

I was pleased to see that I had thrown him off balance. "A date? That has a quaint sound, 'I've got a date.' Who with?"

"Ron Winstead. Do you know him?"

Stu snorted. "I thought you had better taste."

I looked at my shoes. "Well, he asked me. I like to go places now and then, you know. To the movies, out to dinner, that kind of thing."

"You want me to take you out to some dumb movie? Is that what you're telling me?"

"That would be nice," I said.

"Don't go to the pool hall, take me out to the movies. You know what you sound like? You sound like a wife."

I leaned back on my hands and laughed up at him.

"That wasn't supposed to be a compliment."

"I thought it was funny. I'm not allowed to laugh?"

"You know something, Lang? You're changing."

"So, you're not?"

"All right, I'll take you to the movies, if that's what you want," he said. He got back on the cycle, pulled the goggles up over his eyes, and with an explosion of backfiring, he took off down the street.

I sat on the curb feeling my stomach tightening inside me. Ploy #3 from the *Glamour* article, "How To Make the Man You Love Sit Up and Take Notice" had worked like a charm, but I didn't feel as happy about that as I had expected. What difference did it make whether or not Stu took me to the movies if all the time he was with me his heart was roaming the crooked streets of Boomer Hill?

Chapter Four

I wouldn't like to ask you to betray a confidence," Mama began uncomfortably. "But Mary is beside herself, and she pleaded with me to ask you, so I promised I would. Honey, do you know where Stu is staying?"

I looked up at her. "He's not at home? But I just saw him there yesterday."

"Oh, he's still living at home, I suppose. Technically, anyway. But the problem is that lately he isn't coming in at night half the time. And he won't say where he's been. Mary says he scarcely speaks to the family at all. You don't know where he can be going, do you?"

"Boomer Hill, I suppose," I said. I began flipping the top of the salt shaker with my thumb.

"Boomer Hill?" she said, stunned. "What can he be doing over there? Are you sure?"

"He's got friends over there. There's an old blind trumpet player named John Handy that he goes to see."

"You think he's staying with this trumpet player?"

"No," I said. "I think he's probably staying with some woman. Maybe more than one woman."

"He actually told you about this?"

"Sort of. Not directly. But from what he's said, I got the drift." I got up and put my cup and saucer in the dishwasher. Since I had found out about Stu's secret life, he had begun to talk to me a lot about Boomer Hill. It had become, in my mind, a scarred landscape of bright, grotesque characters. As clearly as if I had seen them myself, I could picture the people who lived there—the skinny ex-mathematics professor who jogged the streets in gym shorts, his German shepherd on a leash, talking back to voices that only he could hear; the blind trumpet player sitting on his decayed front porch at dusk, his eyes rolling to the side, his belly overhanging his belt; the skinny girl in a red satin dress who hung out by the little grocery store with the RC Cola sign; and the old man who pulled a wagon full of aluminum cans he had collected, shuffling patiently along in dusty shoes. I had no idea whether the picture I imagined was at all like the real Boomer Hill; I figured it was probably flavored by Stu's love of the bizarre. But I certainly had never had the nerve to go check out the details.

"He's always asking me to come along with him," I said. "To get a taste of real life."

"Dear Lord," said Mama. "What an idea!"

"On his motorcycle," I added.

"His motorcycle!"

"You don't have to worry about me doing it, Mama."

"Of course not. It's not you I'm worried about, Lang. I don't think I'll tell Mary about this," she said. "It would be different if you knew these things for a fact, but—why add to poor Mary's worries? It's not as if there's anything she could do. The truth is they don't have any control over Stu and haven't for years."

"It's their own fault," I said. "If they hadn't kept locking him out of the house every time he wouldn't do what they wanted, it might not even have occurred to him to look for some other place to stay."

"Maybe so," said Mama, "but just think about it a minute, Lang. What kind of parent do you think would have been good for Stu?"

When she put it that way I could see what she meant. Stu's instinct to kick over the traces lived so deep inside him that it was hard to imagine any parent he could have gotten along with.

"Of course, it won't be long until he'll be going away to school," said Mama. "That may solve their problem right there. Going away from home can make such a difference in a person."

Going, going, gone, I thought sadly. It had not escaped my notice that shortly Stu would be leaving for college.

Nobody had been more surprised than the Saranins when St. Bartolph's, a fairly good private college in the mountains, had accepted Stu. His high SAT scores, tapes of his songs, and the enthusiastic recommendations of his language and music teachers, had induced St. B.'s to overlook his grades. Stu had told me that when the acceptance came, his father had said, "It's not Princeton, but I guess it could have been worse." Stu said his parents were looking forward to getting rid of him. If they were, I supposed he could hardly blame them.

"I just hope he hasn't contracted some dreadful disease over in that slum," said Mama. "Anyone will tell you the place is a hotbed of pathology—drug addiction, disease and I don't know what all.''

I heard a familiar little toot out front.

"Speak of the devil," said Mama, glancing out the window.

I ran to open the front door, and there stood Stu. The hot weather had forced him to trade his black leather pants for jeans, but he was still wearing his gloves. He pretended to be indifferent to all warnings about the dangers of motorcycles, but I noticed he never rode without leather gloves to protect his hands in case of a spill. He was very particular about his hands because of playing the piano.

"Hi," I said.

"Only six days, eight hours and thirty-seven minutes and I'm out of this stinking burg," he said, walking on in.

Mama stepped out of the kitchen. "Hi, Stu," she said in a faint voice. I knew she was thinking about what I had told her.

I hastily dashed into the kitchen and grabbed some soft drinks out of the refrigerator. "We'll go on back to my room, Mama," I said, backing out with my arms full of drinks and corn chips. Mama mouthed some silent warning at me that I couldn't make out. Probably she was saying I should leave the door open or spray the place with Lysol after Stu left or something.

Stu and I at once retired to my sitting room. I stole a glance at him under my lashes as I put the corn chips and drinks down on the table. I wanted to ask why he had quit coming home at night, but I knew he would never tell me. "Since it's so close to time for you to leave, I guess you've got a lot of goodbyes to say," I said.

"I'm not into goodbyes. You know that." He tugged on the aluminum loop of the can until it gave off a soft pop. "I want to celebrate my escape from Siler Falls. What do you say? I'll take you out to dinner, even. Saturday night."

"I'd like that. Aren't you even a little bit sad about leaving, Stu?"

"You've got to be kidding."

"You won't even miss your friends over at Boomer Hill?" It was hard for me to even speak of Boomer Hill because jealousy burned painfully in me whenever I thought of the way the Hill seemed to draw him farther and farther away from me.

"Friends?" he said, looking at me in surprise. "I don't have any friends over there."

"What about the girls you told me about?"

He upended the can and took a long drink. It was sensuous somehow just to watch the muscles working in the curve of his long pale throat as he swallowed. Stu had a way of doing something simple and ordinary like swallowing so that you couldn't drag your eyes off of him. His tongue flicked out to lick a drop of liquid off the corner of his mouth. Then he put the can down on the coffee table with a clunk. "Oh, girls," he said. "I thought you said friends."

"Well, what about John Handy?"

"What that man can do with a plunger mute has been a revelation to me," he said, his eyes suddenly burning. He began to pace the floor. "God, he can play."

"Aren't you going to miss him?"

He shrugged.

"Why do you have to act that way?"

"What way?"

"Hard, macho, like nothing can ever touch you. It's such an act."

"I don't think I'm acting," he said. "What you do, Lang, is you take what you see of me and then you add what you know of yourself to it and you think that's the real me. You've got it all wrong. With me, what you see is what you get."

"Okay, then if you don't care about anybody or anything, why do you keep coming around here?"

"Hey, come on," he protested. He pulled a harmonica out of his pocket and began playing. The reedy whine of the thing seemed to fill the room, and my first impulse was to scream at him to answer me. Then I recognized the tune. He was playing, "Baby, I Need Your Loving." I burst out laughing. All my determination to have an honest confrontation seemed to ooze right out my toes.

He stopped playing and looked at the harmonica with satisfaction. "Not bad, huh? I learned to play it from a guy who lives over on Jackson Street. He says it's the best instrument in the world, besides being the only one you can play in handcuffs."

I knew for a fact that sweet Mrs. Hansen had patiently taught Stu piano for years. And he had studied the trumpet under a man who was on the faculty at Siler Falls Christian College. But in Stu's personal mythology, those patient people sank without a trace. I had noticed before that he liked to think he'd picked up all his musical skills from hobos and ex-cons.

He lifted the harmonica to his mouth again and began making it sound like a train. First it was chugging along and then he punctuated the chugs with a mournful whistle. It was an incredibly clever train impersonation, and I grinned.

"Can't you hear that outbound train?" he asked softly. "It's come for me."

That knocked the smile right off my face. I was missing Stu already, and he hadn't even gone. It was as if I needed to rehearse his departure, go over it again and again in my mind to get myself ready for it. He was leaving Siler Falls the way a rocket finally escapes the tug of the earth's atmosphere, in a blast of rebellion. Disappearing into a place I didn't know. Eluding my grasp again.

The evening before Stu was to leave for college, it rained. I watched from the long, tall window in the foyer as drizzle leaked from the dark sky and made dark spatters on the gray wood of the front deck. I turned and got an umbrella out of the coat closet behind me. The grandfather clock by the closet pinged six-thirty. He was late.

I took the furled umbrella up to the front door and looked out again. The drops were coming down more steadily now. I could see them streaking the steel sculpture that stood on the front deck.

"I thought you'd be gone by now, honey," said Mama, stepping onto the parquet floor of the foyer.

Dad pulled her raincoat out of the coat closet and held it out for her.

"Stu's late," I said. "He was supposed to be here at six."

"Maybe it slipped his mind," she said. "Have you called him?"

"I didn't get any answer."

"Why don't you come along with us," suggested Dad. "If he's that late you should teach him a lesson. The next time he won't be late."

"I don't like to do that on his very last night at home," I said. I scuffed the toe of one of my kid sandals against the instep of the other. "He might have just got held up somewhere."

"Are you sure you don't want to go along with us?" asked Mama.

I shook my head.

Giving me sympathetic looks, they ducked their heads and rushed out into the rain.

After they had driven off, I stood at the tall window for some minutes listening to the ticking of the grandfather clock, seized with the ever growing conviction that Stu was over on Boomer Hill somewhere. Carousing probably.

When the hands of the clock clicked into place at six-forty-five, I turned on my heel and went back to my room. I kicked off my high-heeled sandals, scarcely noticing as they flew across the room and lodged behind my cedar chest. Then I began stripping off my bone-colored panty hose, swearing as my fingernail sprung a run in them.

After I had gotten into jeans and a shirt, I grabbed my car keys and headed toward the garage through the kitchen. I knew I had to get out. Anything would be better than sitting alone in the house listening to the rain and feeling sorry for myself. Stu had said he wasn't much into goodbyes. I supposed this was proof of it.

I reminded myself that possibly he'd had a flat tire and hadn't been able to get to the phone. There were dozens of reasonable explanations for his not showing up. But whatever the reason was, there was no good in thinking about it now. It would only make me feel hot and angry all over again.

I backed the car out of the dark garage and into the steady rain. I would go by the drive-in window at Wendy's and get a plain cheeseburger. Then maybe I would just drive around. I could have gone over to Rudene's but I wasn't sure I wanted sympathy. The problem with sympathy was that it might make me feel even more pathetic and left behind than I did already.

My windshield wipers clicked from left to right with relentless rhythm, and I could hear the water hissing under my wheels as I drove out of our neighborhood and turned into the traffic of Vine Street. In front of Safeway, a boy in a yellow slicker was pushing a long line of stacked grocery carts out of the parking lot toward the covered walkway in front of the store. The skies had grown so dark that both Safeway and Gardiner's Barbecue were fully lit, bright rectangular baubles in the rain. A black woman was standing on the corner in a pleated plastic rain hat, waiting for the bus.

I stopped the car when the light turned yellow at the corner of Tenth and Vine and watched as all the traffic signals up the avenue changed to red, casting liquid red light on the wet cars and the streets. Suddenly there was a tearing, roaring sound, and a motorcycle pulled up in the left lane beside me.

Stu was astride the bike, his leather pants slick with rain, and his black hair plastered to his forehead. He looked in my direction and sketched a wave in the air.

I rolled down my window. "Stu Saranin, are you out of your mind?" I yelled.

"Hey, Lang? Whatcha up to?" He grinned.

I didn't answer but turned sharply into the Wendy's parking lot directly ahead. Stu's motorcycle followed me into the lot, roaring and spitting like a chain saw. The side windows of my car were beginning to fog up, and I couldn't see out very well, but all at once the passenger's door opened, and Stu fell onto the front seat beside me, oozing water. At once the entire car seemed filled with his warmth and with the smell of wet leather, beer and sweat. He was such an over-powering presence that it was as if the Mazda had quit being a neat suburban car and had suddenly become the den of something as wild and gamy as a grizzly bear. He shook his wet curls, flinging drops of water against me, and then began peeling off his gloves.

With a kind of detached interest, I saw that my hand was trembling on the steering wheel. I was so angry my tongue felt thick and I wasn't sure I could speak. "Where were you?" I asked. "You were supposed to be at my house at six."

He looked at me blankly for a minute. "Forgot," he said simply. His smile was the sweet, simple smile of a friendly child.

"You are drunk."

"Nah," he said. "Not drunk. Just celebrating. Just celebrating a *little* bit."

I could feel tears stinging at my lashes. "You never think about anybody but yourself. You are so beastly, miserably, stinking selfish I can't stand it. And on top of that you are as drunk as a coot. It's disgusting. Get out of my car. Get out now."

He frowned. "Don't have to get mad, Lang. I didna do anything."

I screamed at him. "I hate you, Stu Saranin. I never want to see you again, do you hear me?" I shoved him out of the car. I heard a slight squooshing sound as he landed flat on the wet asphalt of the parking lot. I felt a twinge of remorse and hoped I hadn't hurt him. When I leaned over to pull the door closed, I saw him out there sitting on the pavement, leaning back on his

hands and looking up at me with a puzzled expression. The rain was streaming down his face. I slammed
the door closed, choking on a sob. As angry as I was,
I knew that if I stayed there a minute longer I would
end up helping him up off the ground, so I drove away
quickly. Driving back toward home I had a lump in my
throat so painful that I couldn't swallow.

Chapter Five

It was months later that I woke up at dawn one morning with the strong feeling that something was wrong. Then I remembered that Stu was dead.

Dead, I thought blankly. All the times I had wondered about what the two of us would be like when we grew up, it had never occurred to me that Stu might not live to grow up. I still couldn't quite hold on to the idea. I half expected even now to hear the roar of his bike in front of the house. I lay in bed staring at the ceiling until I knew for sure that I was not going to be able to get back to sleep. Then I got up and dressed. I could tell I needed to do something to shake off this feeling I had. I made my bed, tucking the sheets up in neat hospital-style corners and looked around the room for something else I could do before breakfast. But my dresser was dusted, my underwear was folded in neat stacks and my homework had been done for hours.

I decided to clean out my car. That was something I hardly ever got around to, and if the work didn't make me feel better, then at least I would have a clean car to show for my effort.

Moving quietly so as not to waken Mama and Dad, I went out to the garage. There I switched on the single bulb that sat high on the rafters, opened my car door and began groping under the front seat for the whisk broom. The air in the garage was cold and stale.

After I swept grit out of the carpet, I pulled out a few gum wrappers that had gotten wedged between the seats. Next I lifted up the front seat to clean under the cushions. There, crumpled in the shadows was something that made my heart stop. I picked it up and draped it over my left hand. It was a black leather glove, wrinkled at the finger joints and still fitted to the shape of Stu's hand. It must have been lying there since that night I pushed him out the car. As eloquent as a gesture, that glove seemed to speak of tapered white fingers and music. And Stu.

I took it inside the house and put it away in my dresser drawer. Then I sat on my bed a minute, trying to catch my breath. I remembered reading that according to physicists there was no reason why time could not go backward as well as forward. Theoretically, it was possible. There was no logical reason why not. Any minute the ceiling of the Sistine Chapel might drop back onto Michelangelo's palette, the giant sequoias might slowly shrink into saplings and then zipper themselves tightly once more into seeds. And Stu might walk into the room, drawl "Don't be ridiculous, Lang," and pull the leather glove over his long fingers.

I heard Mama and Dad's alarm go off in their bedroom and forced myself to rise and go into the kitchen. I filled the coffee pot with water and plugged it in, then I took a bran muffin out of the freezer and put it in the microwave on a paper towel.

Mama tottered into the kitchen, yawned and peered nearsightedly out the kitchen window. Her sandy hair stood out fluffily around her pink face, and there were still creases on her cheek where it had lain pressed against the pillow, so that she looked like a newly wakened baby. She picked up her glasses off the windowsill and pushed them up on the bridge of her nose. "Mercy, look at that fog," she said. "I can barely see as far as the street. It's terrible. I want you to be especially careful driving to school, Lang.''

"It's probably just bad in patches," I said. I tried to butter my muffin, but the pat of butter was so cold and hard the muffin shattered into crumbs in my hand. You would think someone would make a muffin that wouldn't self-destruct before it got to your mouth, I thought bitterly. You couldn't depend on anything anymore. I scooped the crumbs off the plate and ate them with a spoon.

A few minutes later, when I was pulling out of the driveway to go pick up Rudene, I was careful to turn my lights on and go slowly. I had good reason to be thinking how easy it was to get killed.

The fog was particularly bad on the road that ran between the plowed fields going out toward Rudene's. It was eerie to be surrounded by white mist, so that only the glow of headlights showed where cars were approaching in the left lane. In places the road was clear, but before I had a chance to turn off my lights my car would plunge back into fog again, so I had to find the turnoff to Harper's Road mostly by intuition.

I pulled the car up in front of Rudene's trailer, blew the horn and looked around me at the mist. A mailbox was revealed here, a stalk of weeds there, as if the fog were purposely uncovering these bits and pieces to point up their hidden symbolic meaning. It made me feel that if I had been clever enough I could have made sense out of life from the clues that lay all around me.

I could see Rudene's trailer well enough from where I stood, but the other trailers and the sheds and fields behind were shrouded in fog. The sunlight ricocheted between the suspended drops of water and blotted out everything with a glowing whiteness.

Then I noticed a brighter spot in the fog, a single headlight burning in the mist behind and to the left of the trailer. I stared as it moved mysteriously, without any apparent agency, like fox fire. But as I watched, a dark form began to take shape around the light. I saw a black tire and high arched handlebars and could feel my body growing rigid when I made out that what I was looking at was a dark figure on a motorcycle.

"I don't believe in ghosts," I said out loud.

"What did you say?" asked Rudene, opening the car door.

Suddenly a roar of noise exploded in the mist, and the motorcycle charged out onto the road and was gone.

"Who was that?" I said, clenching and unclenching my clammy fingers.

"Who?" said Rudene. She was throwing her books into the back seat.

"Didn't you see the motorcycle?" For a fraction of a second I was afraid she was going to say that she hadn't.

"Oh, you mean Chris," she said. "He really can kick up a racket, can't he? He's supposed to push the bike out to the road and start it out there so he doesn't go scaring people half out of their skins. It's pretty bad when he starts it right up next to somebody's trailer and they're in the shower or sleeping or something. But I guess he doesn't always remember."

"Chris?"

"My cousin, Chris, remember? I told you about him."

"I remember. The one who saw Stu's accident."

Stu would never have believed he would die. "I never died," he would have said. "When my bike crashed, my spirit entered into Chris's body. Don't laugh, Lang. There's a lot going on you don't understand."

"Did I say something funny?" asked Rudene.

I turned on the ignition. "Nope," I said. "I was just thinking." I only wished Stu's crazy ideas had something to them.

As I backed slowly out of the driveway, Rudene leaned out the open window. "Get on out of here, Patches. Shoo! Shoo! That dog just will not mind."

"I'd really like to meet Chris," I said. "Would that be okay?"

"Sure," said Rudene. "He hasn't been here too long, and I bet he'd like to get to know some girls."

When I turned my gaze back to the road ahead, I had the feeling she was looking at me funny, but I was past caring.

At lunchtime Rudene went over to the other side of the cafeteria and got Chris. He came behind her, carrying his tray, and he didn't look a bit cross or embarrassed at being dragged halfway across the cafeteria to join Rudene and me. But when I thought about it, I realized that was typical of Rudene's family. All the Harpers I had ever met were agreeable to a fault.

As he got closer to me I could see why the sight of him on the bike had shaken me. Superficially, he resembled Stu. He was slender with unruly black hair, a square jaw and a firm, slightly cleft chin. In spite of myself, the hair on the back of my neck began to stand on end. I couldn't help thinking that it would be just such a body as this that Stu would have chosen to inhabit, given the chance.

"This is Chris, Lang," said Rudene, plopping back down in her chair.

"Hi," I said.

He smiled at me, and I found my spirits lifting. Just looking at the cleft in his chin and the angular line of that square jaw did something to me I would have found difficult to explain. It was as if I had found out my ticket almost matched the winning ticket in the lottery.

He put his tray down on the table, pulled out a chair and sat down. "It's nice to see a friendly face," he said. "I don't know if you've noticed it but this place is full of stuck-up, narrow-minded jerks."

"I've lived here all my life," I said apologetically.

"You won't have noticed it, then."

"Aw, they're not all jerks, Chris," said Rudene, opening her milk. "You just need to get to know some people better, that's all."

"I guess so," he said, looking directly into my eyes. He had dark brown eyes, darker than bitter chocolate. I sucked in my breath and tried hard to think of the multiplication tables so that I would at least be able to breathe normally.

"Watch out for Chris, Lang," Rudene said. "Because he's not shy one bit. We all figure it's because he's moved around so much."

"Is Lang your real name?" he asked me.

"It's short for Langdon. That's my grandmother's maiden name. But nobody calls me Langdon unless they're mad at me."

"I guess I won't be calling you Langdon, then."

Normally I am put off by boys who come on to me right away, but with Chris it didn't bother me because it was as if we had known each other before.

I looked down at my slice of meat loaf and prodded it with my fork, trying to remember what people said when they sat around cafeteria tables at lunch. "Is SFH a lot different from your old school?" I asked.

"Different? I'll say it is."

"Chris's old school was in California," said Rudene. "You know how it is out there—all those crazy people and weird religions and earthquakes."

"Hey, you're talking about the land of the free, the home of the brave, God's own country. Watch it," said Chris.

"I'd like to visit California someday," I said.

"Me, too," said Chris, looking suddenly gloomy.

"Chris's mom and dad split up," explained Rudene. "It was such a shame. Now Aunt Rachelle lives in Guam, and Uncle Jimmy lives in Hawaii, and both of them got married to other people."

"How did you end up here, then?"

"During the divorce they shipped me off to military school," he explained. "I hated it, so I just took off and came here. I figured they're family. They've got to take me in, right?"

I spotted the slightly wary look of somebody who is hurting and felt a sudden twinge of kinship with Chris.

"Always room for one more," said Rudene. "Chris moved right in with Aunt Molly's boy, Jerry. Jerry's got his own trailer at the back of the lot. It's real nice. Jerry moved back there after Bo was born. Like Aunt Molly says, there are only just so many people who can share the bathroom in the morning when everybody's getting ready for school, and then it gets plain ridiculous."

"How do you like Siler Falls so far?" I asked Chris.

"It's okay, I guess. But have you noticed how there isn't anything to do around here?" asked Chris.

"We now and then have some pretty wild parties," said Rudene, looking at me out of the corner of her eye.

"Not very many wild parties," I said hastily. "Actually, I know just what you mean. A lot of kids complain about not having anything to do. It's pretty much just the movies or the Christian coffee house most weekends, unless you go to Raleigh, and that's a long drive."

"Maybe you'd like to go to the movies with me this weekend," said Chris.

"Sure," I said, "I'd like that." I swallowed. I was wondering what my parents would say when Chris showed up on a motorcycle. When Stu and I had gone out we had always used his parents' car, but I doubted

Chris had a way to borrow a car. I didn't care. I would worry about details later.

"Saturday night? Sevenish?" he asked.

With a sense of relief I realized that my parents would have already left for the symphony by seven. They wouldn't even be there to see Chris arrive on the motorcycle.

"Okay," I said.

"You want to come, too, Rudene?" he asked her.

"What's playing?" asked Rudene. Then, as Chris turned his gaze on her she added hastily, "I don't think I'd better this weekend. I've got a lot of sewing I need to catch up on."

"Too bad," said Chris.

Later on, when Rudene and I were walking back to class, I thanked her for bringing Chris over. "You've saved my life, Rudene. I really appreciate it. I can't tell you."

"Chris seemed to like you right off, didn't he?" she said. "He's real nice, Lang. I don't see why you say he's going to save your life, though. I know you've been sad about Stu and all, but I think you've been doing real well. Aren't you feeling better now than you were at first?"

"Oh, of course. I mean, sure I am," I said. I didn't want to admit to Rudene that since Stu's death it was as if everything about me had gotten a heavy shot of

Novocaine except the pain that never quite went away. You lost him, a nagging voice kept telling me. Now he's gone and it's your fault. I pushed the thought back away down inside of me. Things were going to be different. As soon as I saw Chris I had been sure of it. It was as if I were getting a second chance.

"Chris has been having kind of a bad time of it," confided Rudene. "His folks had one of those real messy divorces where they had detectives following each other around, if you can believe that, and they don't even speak to each other anymore. It's really sad. I don't see why people can't do better than that. And it's awful for Chris. I mean, he's come here, but he hardly knows us, with him moving around the way he has. I think it's kind of lonely for him sometimes."

"Don't you think everybody gets lonely sometimes?" I said.

"Not me," said Rudene.

I sighed. "I wouldn't mind trading places for a while."

"And get my freckles and my D in trig?" She laughed. "Oh, no, you wouldn't."

When we got to class, I wrote on the inside of my notebook "CHRIS." Then, crossword-puzzle style, I wrote under the *S* of Chris's name, "TU" so that the names formed two sides of a triangle, linked by the *S*.

"Would everyone please pass up yesterday's assignment?" said Mr. Crocker.

I quickly scribbled out what I had written and began leafing through my notebook looking for the assignment. I didn't want somebody to see what I had written and decide I had gone completely out of my mind.

Chapter Six

You just get on the bike here, right behind me," explained Chris, "and put your arms around my waist."

"All right," I said, and gulped.

"You'll be fine if you just hold on tight. But watch your legs," he warned. "Keep them up on these pegs. Don't let them touch those exhaust pipes down there or you could get burned."

"I'll be careful." The words sounded ironic to me, considering I was just about to get on a motorcycle.

"Here," he said, handing me a large blue helmet. "Put this on."

"What about you?"

He held up the red one dangling from his other arm by its chin strap. "I've got an extra."

He put on his shiny red helmet and, looking like a huge Martian insect, he threw a leg over the bike.

I fastened my chin strap, took a deep breath and tried to do the same, but instead I ended up sort of scrambling awkwardly up by stepping on the exhaust pipes. When I got on the raised up part of the seat behind Chris, I noticed with dismay that my feet didn't even come close to touching the ground.

I put my feet on the metal pegs that stuck out from the cycle, closed my eyes, put my arms around Chris's waist and held on very tightly.

"That's the way," he said. "Okay, hold on. Here we go."

The bike began to rumble and then to roar. I could feel it vibrating under me. Then it tipped a little, and I knew we were moving.

The wind beat against me with the force of a fire hose. When I got up the courage to open my eyes and peer through the wind visor attached to the helmet, I saw the neighborhood was going by in a blur, and I felt suddenly chilled to the bone with sheer terror. We shot out onto Vine into all the traffic, and I had to screw my eyes closed again because the sight of the huge cars around us made me gasp. I was afraid I would pass out and slide right off the seat. I was scarcely even aware of how close I was to Chris or that I was holding on to him so tightly he might have trouble breathing. My only thought was that I hoped we weren't going to get killed. The wind roared in my ears and beat against me until my skin felt numb. Then the noise of the bike began to subside a little. I could make out the quieter rumble of engines around us and smell exhaust fumes. I opened my eyes and saw that we were pulling up to a stop at a red light. If the car behind us doesn't stop, I thought, we are dead. My mouth got suddenly dry, but a second later the light turned green, and we took off again.

We zoomed right up in front of the Cardinal Theater and the bike rolled to a stop. Chris put his feet down and took off his helmet. "We're here," he said.

"Good," I said faintly.

"You can let go now," he said, looking over his shoulder and grinning at me.

I detached my arms from his waist and then gingerly got off the bike, taking care to avoid the hot exhaust pipes. While Chris dismounted and propped the thing up with its kickstand, I took off my helmet and took a few deep breaths.

"I've never ridden on a motorcycle before," I confessed.

"I kind of guessed that," said Chris.

"Lang?" said a voice behind me.

I turned and saw Suzy Harkness looking at me very closely, as if she were unsure of my identity. I realized that it was just possible I might look strangely zonked out after my ordeal. I certainly felt wobbly on my feet.

"I thought that was you," she said. She was with Mike Taylor, a six-foot-one forward from our basketball team. I hadn't realized that Suzy was going out with him. Come to think of it, this had every sign of a first date. Mike's prominent Adam's apple was moving convulsively with nervousness, and he had made earnest attempts to slick down his blond hair, which had a tendency to stick up in several places.

"Do you two know Chris?" I asked. "He's just moved here from California."

"Hi, Chris," said Suzy.

"Some bike," said Mike, moving over to admire the monster.

"Yeah," said Chris. He stroked its blue nose in a possessive gesture.

"My parents won't let me ride on motorcycles," said Suzy.

"We'd better go on in," I said, avoiding her eyes. "I'd hate to miss the first part of the movie."

"Yo, Lang!" Bobby Miller called. As we went in the door, I turned back and waved at him. I felt exposed, as if searchlights had been trained on me. I was afraid people might be noticing Chris's resemblance to Stu, wondering what it meant. As quickly as I could, I ducked into the lobby.

Inside, Chris was buying a huge tub of buttered popcorn. Holding it under one arm, he pushed open the door to the darkened theater, and I followed him into the anonymity of the darkness. The words "This preview has been approved for all motion picture audiences," were flashing on the screen.

"Good," said Chris. "It hasn't started. Is this row okay?"

We inched down the empty row, and Chris placed the popcorn between us. He settled into his seat and at once put his arm around me. Reaching for a handful of popcorn in a kind of daze, I watched the screen credits begin to roll by, and with a sense of surprise realized I was feeling good. I decided it had something to do with the motorcycle. While I had been whizzing through town on the motorcycle, all my confused feelings about Stu had vanished. Of course, I had been terrified, but I figured that on the whole it was a fair trade-off.

Also, now that I was off of the motorcycle, the relief I felt was incredible. It seemed a privilege to be breathing the canned, air-conditioned air of the theater. It was a rare pleasure to feel Chris's arm pressing against me. I was just plain glad to be alive.

"I can see how riding a motorcycle could get addictive," I murmured into Chris's ear. "I mean, anytime you had anything you didn't want to think about you could hop on the bike and it'd be presto zonko, no thoughts at all."

"Are there a lot of things you don't want to think about?"

"Some," I said cautiously.

"Shhh," said someone behind us.

We sat engrossed in the movie until at length the villains in the plot were routed and we had polished off the last few greasy crumbs of popcorn. Filmy curtains began to draw closed over the screen, and the faint sound of shuffling feet was heard all over the theater.

"Why don't we get something to eat?" Chris said.

"How about Hardee's?" I said. "It's right across the street."

"Right. We could even walk," said Chris, winking at me.

We crossed the street with the crowd and walked into the warmth of Hardee's, with its overpowering smell of hamburgers and french fries. I was hoping that nobody I knew would come over to talk to Chris and me. I wanted to look at his face and try to recapture that feeling that I was almost in touch with Stu.

Chris led the way to a booth on the quiet side of the restaurant. "Is here okay?" he asked.

"This is perfect," I said, looking around. There were only two booths on the side Chris had picked.

"You better stay here and keep our place. There's a pretty big crowd still coming in. I'll go get the stuff. What do you want?"

"French fries and a Coke, I guess."

"Be right back."

This side of the Hardee's had always been my favorite. It was more private and it had certain scenic advantages. From our booth you could see through a glass window right into the kitchen where the hamburgers were being broiled. You also got to look overhead and watch the maneuverings of a kind of makeshift food trolley that served the drive-in window.

When he got back with our food, Chris saw me watching it.

"This place has the slowest drive-thru window in town," I told him proudly. "See, first the people in the car have to send the money up and over on the trolley. And then the kitchen has to send the food and the change back."

"Quite a show. Maybe they should have a cover charge," he said.

Chris took the top off his bun and examined his hamburger. "You know something, Lang? I think you're naturally cut out for small-town life."

"I guess you think all this stuff about the trolley is pretty boring."

"Absolutely not. Do I look bored? Look, I think simple pleasures are great. No kidding. Get your kicks where you can."

I could feel chills down my back as if I had plunged into an ice bucket. But probably lots of boys had voices that took on a husky edge now and then, I told myself. And if Chris had no touch of the South on his vowels, no Siler Falls twang, it was because he had moved around so much. That was why. It was being uprooted that made a person talk like a television announcer. As for Stu, the reason he didn't have an accent was that his parents were from up North, and he grew up in the South so his speech was poised in the never land between the two. There was a perfectly logical explanation for the similarity between Chris's and Stu's voices if I just thought it all out.

"Do you believe in the transmigration of souls?" I asked suddenly.

"Listen, you ought not to take all that stuff Rudene said about California seriously. It's not really true that California is full of flakes. Sure, there are some flakes, but that's the way it is everywhere."

"I didn't mean to be hinting that you were strange," I said, embarrassed. "I just used to know somebody who was interested in that kind of thing, that's all. That's the only reason I asked."

"Well, no, I don't. Do *you* believe in the transmigration of souls?"

"Oh, no! Besides, when you think about it, how would you even know whether a soul had migrated or not? It's ridiculous. I don't know why I brought it up."

He grinned. "I know how you'd tell," he said. "Like if my soul migrated into somebody else's body, the poor sucker would wake up one morning and say, 'Man, I gotta have a Harley-Davidson XLH 1100.'"

I hesitated. "You don't happen to play a musical instrument, do you?"

"Trumpet," he said, biting into his hamburger. "Why?"

"If your soul migrated into somebody else's, maybe he would play—" I swallowed hard "—the trumpet, too."

"Could be," he said. "Okay, you tell me. If your soul migrated, what would it take along with it?"

"I don't think my soul is the adventurous type," I said.

"It would refuse to go, huh? Well, maybe it's got the right idea. I think it's better to stay put. If you can," he said grimly.

"You couldn't live with your mother or your father?" I asked sympathetically. "Wouldn't that be better than living here in Jerry's trailer?"

"No," he said. "It'd be like World War III with Mom telling me what a creep Dad is and getting me to nag him about the support payments, and Dad telling me what a loser Mom is and how everything that's wrong with me is her fault. Meanwhile, these new people they married would be looking at me like something the exterminator missed on his last visit. Forget it. I just feel sorry for Samantha. She's too little to get out of there. She's actually starting to call that creep Mom married 'Daddy.' Don't get me started. I sound like a lunatic. Actually, you'd never know it, but normally I'm a very nice, easygoing guy. I'm just a little thrown off balance by the disintegration of my unhappy home, that's all. It's kind of like living on an island where the natives are at war, you know? You keep dodging arrows and you think you've got it bad, but then the island starts sinking and you see you didn't know when you were well off."

"It sounds awful."

"Okay, well, I guess I've told you all my troubles. Now you get to tell me yours."

"I'm getting along all right. No major troubles."

"Must be nice. Have you and Rudene been friends long?"

"Since we were little kids. Rudene taught me how to pump on a swing. She showed me how to make little balls out of the clay under the steps at play school. At the time I thought that was the peak of human achievement. I guess we must have been about four then. We've been friends practically forever."

"Maybe that explains it."

"Explains what?"

"Why you two seem so different. If I asked Rudene to tell me her troubles she'd be going on a mile a minute about trig and how her hair frizzes and how she wants to put on ten pounds, and all the time she'd be looking happy as a clam. I ask you about your troubles, and you say everything's great, and you sit there looking as if your best friend died. Hey, did I say something wrong?"

"Excuse me," I said, reaching for a napkin. "I think something got in my eye."

He reached for my hand. "Hey, that's okay," he said. "What's the matter?"

"Sorry," I said. I was wondering if I was going to have to make a mad dash to the ladies' room, where I could sob uncontrollably in private. "It's just that my best friend did die."

"My God, I'm sorry. I didn't know."

"It's okay. It's fine, really. Sometimes it hops up and catches me off guard, that's all. I don't want to talk about it. Honestly. So, uh, that was really a fun movie, wasn't it?"

He looked at me a little uneasily, but withdrew his hand. "Let's blow this place."

During the ride home, I actually opened my eyes some and watched the lights of Vine Avenue whizzing by us. "Are you cold?" Chris yelled back at me.

"Freezing!" I shouted.

"Want me to slow down some?"

"No, I like it." I held on tight to Chris and let the fear and the icy wind drench me. We turned off of Vine and zoomed downhill into my neighborhood. I felt free. I felt as if I could have ridden to China on that bike and have been the better for it.

We zoomed up into my family's driveway, and the bike rolled to a stop in front of the garage. "Looks like your parents are home," said Chris. "There's a light on."

"No, that's in my room," I said. "I must have left my desk lamp on."

I was thankful that my parents were not home. It was better for all concerned if they just didn't find out about Chris's bike.

He helped me down. Then, as soon as my feet touched the ground, he put his arms around me. I could feel his breath warm on my icy cheeks. "Lang," he said, "will you be my woman?"

I gaped at him in astonishment.

He looked at me thoughtfully. "Too soon, huh?"

"I'll say!"

"Worth a try," he said, grinning at me.

I pushed him away. "I had a lovely time," I said.

"Sure," he said. He walked with me up to the front door, then held out his hand and formally shook hands with me. As I turned to let myself in with my key, I was struck by an uncomfortable thought. Chris was a bit of a clown. I hadn't expected that.

Chapter Seven

It was days later that the storm caused by my going out with Chris broke over my head. When I came in from school Tuesday afternoon, I dropped my books in my sitting room and went into the kitchen to get myself something to eat. Mama was sitting at the table and looked up at me, her face crumpled with anxiety.

"Sweetheart, Lydia Harkness tells me Suzy saw you riding on a motorcycle Saturday night. What can she be talking about?"

I don't know why it hadn't occurred to me that the news about the motorcycle would somehow get back to my parents. I took a breath. "Well, Chris has a motorcycle."

"Is Chris the boy you went out with Saturday night? I still don't understand why you were riding on his motorcycle."

"That's what he drives. He doesn't have a car."

"But darling, after everything that's happened—" She broke off, her face working. "I didn't think we would have to say anything. We've always agreed about how dangerous motorcycles were. What can be going on with you?"

"I just wanted to do it. Lots of people ride on them." I ran my fingers through my hair. I hardly even knew what I was saying to Mama. I was only trying to clear a little personal space where I could work things out for myself.

"Sweetheart, you know we just want to help," said Mama. "I've talked to your dad about this, and he and I agree that maybe, if you're upset, you know, you might need to talk to someone. A specialist. Someone who could help you. Your father knows of some very good—"

"I do not need to see a psychiatrist. Honestly, I am the only girl in town whose parents would send her to a psychiatrist because she rode on a motorcycle. Listen to yourself, Mama."

"I want you to promise me you won't ride on this boy's motorcycle again, Lang. If you don't want to go talk to anybody, all right, but I can't stand by and let you ruin your life and end up paralyzed or even dead, like Stu."

"Stop it!" I shouted.

"I'm sorry to upset you, but I shouldn't even have to be saying this. It should be obvious on the face of it. Will you promise me you won't do this again?"

I looked up at the ceiling so that I didn't have to look at her face. "Okay, I promise," I said.

I went to my room. I wasn't hungry anymore anyway.

When Dad got in that evening he came into my sitting room. "Hey, sweetheart," he said. "Did you and your mother talk?" He was looking at my face as if he were searching for the diagnostic signs of some deadly disease.

"I told her I wouldn't ride on Chris's motorcycle anymore."

"Good. Now have you given any thought to going to talk to somebody about this? You know, it's no disgrace to get help when you need it. All of us can stand sometimes to talk our troubles over with other people. I know of a very good man—"

"I said I wouldn't ride the motorcycle anymore. Isn't that enough? Would you leave me alone?" I ran into my bedroom and slammed the door. Then I sat on the bed looking out the window and thinking there was something crazy going on with my life. I seemed to be getting more and more like Stu. If I began by riding motorcycles and went on to start fighting with my parents, was hanging around pool halls in Boomer Hill going to come next?

That night at dinner Mama and Dad and I were all very polite to each other.

"Would you please pass the sweet potatoes, dear?" asked Mama. "How was your day, Steven?"

"Hectic, as usual. I don't know how that new girl is going to work out. She's a whiz at getting insurance forms out, but her typing is awful. How's the prom decoration committee coming, Lang?"

"Fine, I guess. We've got enough chicken wire, anyway." One of the great issues of our time, I thought sourly. Prom decorations.

I began to think enviously of Chris, who was roughing it with Jerry in the trailer. *He* didn't have to make chitchat with parents who kept evaluating his mental health with their every glance. I wished Chris were with me right then instead of my two very nervous parents. No, I wished I were zooming all over Siler Falls on that motorcycle of his, smelling the honeysuckle on vacant lots and splashing through puddles green with pollen. I wanted to be speeding smack through the center of Boomer Hill, going past those bars and those skinny dogs scratching themselves on street corners. "Let me show you life," Stu had said. Well, it still wasn't too late for me to see it. I wasn't dead.

That night I knew I was going to have trouble sleeping and, sure enough, at midnight I was lying in bed watching patterns on the wall made by the moon shining through the venetian blinds.

Wouldn't it be funny, I thought, if it were my body that Stu had transmigrated into and I didn't even realize it? I would end up like Alice when she fell down the rabbit hole and kept testing herself on the multiplication tables to make sure she hadn't turned into Mabel, the class dumbbell. Only in my case I would have to use some other kind of test since Stu and I both had the multiplication tables down pat. I would have to try to play the trumpet, for example, or see what poetry I could recite. Stu knew the entire *The Rubáiyát of Omar Khayyám* by heart. It was just the sort of thing he liked—full of dark philosophy, futility and endless upended glasses of wine. I wondered how much of it I could remember? I recited softly:

"The Moving Finger writes; and, having writ,
Moves on: nor all your Piety nor Wit
Shall lure it back to cancel half a Line,
Nor all your Tears wash out a Word of it."

My eyes had begun to swim with tears when suddenly a loud crack rang against my window. The breath knocked out of me by the surprise of it, I could barely manage to sit. Slowly I raised the blind. No wind was stirring outside. It was perfectly still. I made out a dark figure below on the moon-washed lawn.

"Lang! It's Chris!"

I stared down at him, feeling a thud of disappointment. "Just a minute, Chris," I called. My voice sounded hoarse to my ears.

Jumping up, I quietly drew open a drawer and began pulling on jeans and a sweatshirt. I didn't bother with underwear, but it didn't feel right going down to talk to Chris in my nightgown. I slipped sneakers onto my bare feet, then tiptoed out on the deck and down the long stairs to the lawn. I felt as if I were honoring some ritual that had lost its meaning. It must be, I thought, in this same faintly hopeful way that priests say mass after they have lost their faith.

When I reached the foot of the stairs, Chris was there waiting for me. "I was afraid your mom and dad were going to hear me," he said. "Lucky thing I remembered which room was yours. You wouldn't happen to want to go out and get something to eat, would you?"

Did I want to go out to eat or did I want to go back to my room and count the stripes of moonlight on my wall? No contest. "I'd love to. I can't seem to get to sleep," I said.

"Me either. It's this dumb moon. I don't know how people hack it when they live in the land of the midnight sun. The midnight moon is bad enough."

Chris pushed the bike down the street a way before starting it up so as to be sure not to wake my parents. Then I hopped on behind him, and the bike began to shudder under us. Its halogen lamp cast a column of light ahead of us into the night as we roared up the street in the direction of Vine. I was old enough to take motorcycle rides at midnight if I wanted to, I told myself, but a younger, guiltier part of me was feeling like a criminal. I was hoping fervently that we wouldn't run into anybody my parents knew.

When we got to McDonald's on Vine I was relieved to see that the only person inside was a truck driver drinking black coffee out of a cardboard cup. Luckily, none of my parents' friends had been seized tonight by a sudden craving for Chicken McNuggets.

Chris and I moved up to the Formica counter where a skinny girl stood taking orders, and Chris asked for a chocolate shake. "Milk helps you sleep," he told me. "It's a scientific fact. No kidding."

"A chocolate shake for me, then, too."

I could feel the seams of my jeans against my bare skin, and I began to wish I had taken time to put on my underwear. It undeniably gave me a strange feeling to be at McDonald's in the middle of the night knowing I was only half-dressed.

We gathered our milkshakes, straws and napkins and sat down at a booth. Chris raised his shake to me in a mock toast and clicked his cup against mine.

"Two lives drawn together by insomnia," he said. "I knew we were going to have a lot in common. Have you reconsidered about being my woman?"

"That sounds to me like a proposition you don't make a girl on the second date."

"It gets your attention, though, doesn't it?" he said cheerfully. "Besides, who's counting? Don't you feel as if we've known each other in another life?"

I stared at him.

He coughed uncomfortably. "That was a popular line back where I used to live," he explained.

I looked at his chin, at the line of his jaw, but nothing happened to me at all.

"Do I have a spot of egg on my chin or something?" he asked.

"I'm sorry. I guess I must be in a daze."

"You're getting sleepy."

"I guess so."

"Let's get you home, then."

We dumped our half-finished shakes in the trash barrel and walked out into the cool night air. As I was clambering up on the bike again, Chris said, "I had a feeling about you."

I shot a startled glance at my Levi's but every seam was intact. Nobody could possibly have guessed that I wasn't wearing underwear.

Chris threw his leg over the bike and spoke over his shoulder. "I mean, not every girl would do this, you know," he said.

"I'm an idiot all right," I said. I was thinking about how I had promised Mama I wouldn't ride on Chris's bike. By now I was feeling a whole lot less like a free spirit and more like a victim of temporary insanity.

"You know I didn't mean that. I think it's terrific that you'd come out and get a shake with me. It was kind of fun, wasn't it?"

I had to admit that it certainly beat lying in my bed crying.

"To tell you the truth, I get kind of lonely at night sometimes," said Chris, looking a little sheepish. "I ride by these houses and see people inside watching television, and I wish I were in there with them. With a family, you know? Or just somebody to talk to whenever I wanted."

I put my arms around his waist and leaned my cheek against his back. "I know," I said. "There seems to be a lot of that going around lately. Chris, let's not go back just yet. Let's just swing around town a little bit."

He shot me a surprised look over his shoulder. "Sure. I've got a full tank. Get on that helmet."

I fastened the helmet on my head and then grabbed on to him again. The bike growled and trembled under us, then we tore out of the parking lot. The town was sleeping. Only a few lights had been left burning at the Professional Office Building and Gardiner's Barbecue, as if the buildings had been switched to automatic pilot for the night. I noticed that a couple of cars were parked in front of the darkened Safeway, probably curbside marijuana dealers at work.

We tore on past the street that ran into my neighborhood and instead headed east of town, where the buildings began to peter out into a few odd stores stationed along the highway. Something white streaked across the road ahead of us and dived with round haunches into the brush, a cat out hunting. The moon was high in the sky and so bright it seemed to stand out from the night, as if it were an illustration in a pop-up book. We roared by the dark hulk of the saddle shop, where pitch-colored ropes were looped over posts outside, then on past woods and fields.

"Honeysuckle," I said.

"Did you say something?" yelled Chris.

"I smell honeysuckle," I yelled back.

"I'm turning around now," he yelled.

"Okay."

He wheeled onto the paved area in front of Discount Shoes, kicking up gravel, then turned back onto the open highway. A few minutes later the headlight of the bike glinted on some dark metal disks nailed to posts at the city limits—the Lions, the Elks and Rotary Club were all welcoming us back to Siler Falls.

We roared back into the city limits down Vine. In front of Safeway we passed a police car. I cringed, but it didn't come after us. After all, I reminded myself, there was no sign on my back reading Runaway Girl.

Minutes later we were coasting soundlessly down the hill into my neighborhood. Chris had switched off the motor.

"'Softly softly catchee monkee,'" he observed.

I giggled. I was beginning to get a little nervous. What would I say if, when I got back home, Mama and Dad were waiting for me with hurt amazement in their eyes?

At the foot of the hill we got off, and Chris pushed the bike the rest of the way. When we got to my house he parked it at the curb and walked with me through the trees to the foot of the deck stairs.

"Good night," I whispered.

I could feel his fingertip rough against my cheek. "Good night," he said. Then he bent and kissed me, drawing me close to him so that, for a moment that seemed suspended out of time, I forgot who he was, and it happened again—that feeling of closeness to Stu. Then Chris's hand was cool on my back, and all at once I remembered I wasn't wearing any underwear. Feeling hot and cold at once from embarrassment, I twisted away from him.

"You aren't mad, are you?" he whispered anxiously.

I shook my head then turned away, and pressing my lips tightly together so I could be sure I wouldn't either laugh or cry, I ran lightly up the stairway.

When I got back to my room, there was no sign that Mama and Dad had heard a thing. I could faintly hear the sound of Dad's snoring down the hall.

I got back in my own bed, feeling queasy, as if I had eaten a huge box of chocolate cremes. I wouldn't have wanted Chris to know the reason I was drawn to him, I realized. I remembered too well myself how it felt to be treated as if I could be easily exchanged for anyone who looked like me. I could recall with painful clarity that girl who looked like me at Stu's funeral.

But in spite of these uncomfortable thoughts, I went to sleep at once, just the same as if I had a clear conscience.

When I got up the next morning, Mama was already in the kitchen. She was sniffling and had left a trail of wadded blue Kleenexes all over the counter. In the distance I could hear Dad singing in the shower. In two minutes he would be wrapped in a towel and carefully brushing his teeth from the gums down. Another typical morning in the Devereaux household.

Mama sneezed. "This dratted pollen," she said. "It's terrible." She reached up into the cabinet and pulled out a box of raisin bran.

"Mama," I said. "I have to tell you something."

"What did you say?" she said. She blew her nose and looked at me over the Kleenex.

"I can't promise you that I won't see Chris."

"I don't understand, Lang."

"I *need* Chris."

Her nose was buried in blue Kleenex but her eyes were looking at me in alarm. "Why don't we discuss this with your father when he comes in."

By the time I had eaten the last crumb of my muffin, Dad was walking into the kitchen in his maroon bathrobe. His hair was wet, and there was a red mark on his neck where he had scraped himself shaving.

"Lang has something she needs to talk to us about," said Mama.

"I was only telling Mama that I couldn't promise not to see Chris again," I said doggedly. "I can't promise because I'm going to see him whatever you say."

"I don't see the problem," Dad said. "Your mother and I have never said you couldn't date Chris, have we, Sara?" Mama's mouth opened, but Dad didn't give her a chance to speak. "We only said you couldn't ride on this Chris's motorcycle."

"What's the difference? A motorcycle happens to be what he drives." I added pugnaciously, "And we always wear helmets, too."

"Protection for the cranium," he commented, "but not for the spinal cord. I don't see why you and Chris can't go anywhere you wish in your car."

"My car? I don't think he'd like that."

"Well, your mother and I don't like the motorcycle," he pointed out mildly. "It seems to me that using your car makes good sense."

"But what if he won't go along with it?"

"He'll go along with it," said Dad, reaching for a muffin. "I would have put up with a lot more than that to go out with a pretty girl like you. Your mother and I aren't going to give in on this matter, Lang. I don't have to tell you why. This is too important. I'm relying on you to be sensible about this."

"Gotta go," I said. I grabbed my books and scooted out to the garage. They couldn't make me, I thought. That was one thing I had learned from Stu. There isn't much people can make you do. But the fact was that even as woozy as I was from lack of sleep, I could see that what they were saying made sense.

Things looked different in the daytime. When I got in my own little car and fastened my seat belt, it seemed impossible to me that only hours before I was zooming out of town on a motorcycle. I wondered if this was what Stu had felt when he had come back from Boomer Hill, a sense that two parts of his life didn't quite mesh. But, I reminded myself, I wasn't going to think about Stu. Whatever happened, I was not going to think about Stu.

Chapter Eight

When I saw Chris heading in my direction in the cafeteria I choked on my milk. I hadn't figured out yet what I was going to say. I was going to have to decide quick whether I was a motorcycle moll or whether I was the careful responsible person I had been my entire life. My ability to decide this was somewhat impaired by a hiccup.

Chris put his tray down next to mine and looked at me with sympathy. "Hiccups, huh?"

I nodded silently because I was hiccuping too hard to speak.

"I can cure hiccups," he said. "I have what you might call a natural gift. Now, hold on for a minute." He filled a teaspoon with sugar and handed it to me. "Best thing in the world for hiccups," he said.

By sucking in my diaphragm I managed to stop hiccuping long enough to swallow the teaspoon of sugar.

"See?" said Chris. "All gone. The theory behind it is that the sugar tickles a hiccup nerve that's at the back of your throat."

At once I was convulsed by another hiccup.

"Yours is a tricky case. But don't worry. Try this. Take a deep breath and I'll tell you when you can let it out."

I obediently sucked in a deep breath, and Chris began studying the second hand on his watch. Just when I thought I might explode, he signaled me to exhale.

I let out my breath with a whoosh. "I'll bet I was turning purple," I said.

"A little purple, maybe," he admitted. "But it was worth it, wasn't it?"

I hiccuped.

"Wait a minute," said Chris. "I'm going to try something else. Hang on, I'll be back in a few minutes."

I sat surveying the food on my tray, hiccuping and thinking dismally about the man I had read about in the *Guinness Book of Records* who had had hiccups for twenty or thirty years. I hoped I wouldn't go down in history as the girl who beat his record.

Suddenly a loud noise exploded behind my left ear. "Eeek!" I shrieked. I levitated several inches out of my chair.

Chris sat down next to me and laid a tattered paper bag on the table. "That ought to do it," he said.

"You practically gave me a heart attack," I said, almost choking.

"But you're over the hiccups, right?"

I sat for a minute waiting for the hiccups to reoccur. "I guess so," I admitted.

He sat down and leaned perilously back in his chair.

"Chris," I said quickly, before I had a chance to change my mind, "I've got to tell you something. I can't ride on the motorcycle anymore. I promised my parents."

He straightened up. "You aren't still mad at me, are you?"

"I'm not mad at you at all. I was never mad at you. It's just that I can't ride with you anymore."

"Not even at midnight?"

"Especially not then."

"I guess this is curtains, then," he said dolefully.

"Goodbye, you mean. This is goodbye."

"If you say so. But I'll miss you."

"No, I mean—" I glared at him in exasperation. "Never mind. You *know* what I mean. We could still go places together. If we wanted to. In my car."

"Okay," he said, brightening. "That could have its advantages. I hear the birth rate of the country rose by thirty per cent after the introduction of the automobile."

"Don't get your hopes up," I said.

"How about we go out for hamburgers Friday night?" he said. "I'll buzz over to your place about six, and we can go in your car if you want."

"Okay," I said. "But I warn you, I'm bringing along a chair and a whip."

Suzy Harkness appeared from nowhere and put her tray down across from me. "What did you say?" she asked, looking at me with wide eyes.

"Lang and I were discussing sexual perversity in modern America—from a purely personal standpoint, you understand," said Chris without missing a beat. "We were saying SFH ought to offer a course in it for all us interested parties."

Suzy looked first at him and then at me with obvious uneasiness. "That sounds extremely interesting," she said. "I've read about that sort of thing."

"It's the lab experiments that would be really interesting," Chris assured her.

"He's joking, Suzy."

"Oh, I knew that," Suzy said, blushing.

I shot a reproachful glance at Chris. He was always catching me by surprise. The things I expected to be tricky were easy with him. And the things I never thought to worry about popped up and clobbered me. I had expected him to go all macho on me and refuse to let me drive him anyplace, but I had certainly not expected him to try to convince Suzy Harkness the two of us were kinky.

It was easy enough to see why I was having this problem of being perpetually caught off balance, I thought. It was not Chris who was haunted by Stu. It was me. I kept expecting him to be like Stu, and he wasn't. He wasn't at all.

"Lang?" said Suzy. "Are you in a trance or something?"

"She's been missing out on a lot of sleep lately," said Chris.

I shot an evil look at him, but he only grinned at me.

"I was just saying," Suzy said, pink with embarrassment, "that I hope you're going to make it to the next work party. Bring a friend. I've started to worry about whether we're going to be able to finish that tunnel in time."

I tried to look as if I shared her concern. After all, I had a certain responsibility to Suzy. I had stuck her with the job of chairman. But the truth was I couldn't work up even a feeble interest in a tunnel made of tissue paper. Maybe I was ready to graduate, after all.

"I understand you're from California," Suzy said to Chris.

"Yup, I was a member of an obscure religious cult there. We respect all forms of life and venerate the skateboard."

"I'm a Methodist myself," said Suzy. "Well, I guess I'd better be going." She picked up her tray, rose and backed away from the table.

"I don't think that girl likes me," Chris observed, as he watched her retreat.

I decided it would probably be possible, with close observation, to make a list of twenty or thirty ways Chris was different from Stu. There were small things like the almost oriental straightness of his hair where Stu's was all loose curls, or the bluntness of his fingers where Stu's were slim and tapered. But what was most different was simply who he was. Now that I was getting to know Chris, that was what I couldn't ignore. He might play the trumpet and ride a motorcycle, but he wasn't like Stu. Not a bit. I supposed that even if a person tried to act like another person on purpose it couldn't be done. The core, the self, whatever you call it, was different. The motives, the impulses and the tastes that made Stu tick could never be duplicated.

"Do you think you can wish something so hard that you almost make it come true?" I asked Chris.

"Absolutely not," he said. "If wishing worked that way we would be zooming down a dirt road on the Harley right now, picking daisies out of our teeth."

"But you can wish something so hard you almost convince yourself it's true. I know that."

"If you do that you're making a big mistake. It's better to face up to whatever it is you're up against. I guess there's not a chance you're going to tell me what you're talking about, is there?" he said. "I've never known anybody who came out less with what was on her mind."

"I was thinking how much at first you reminded me of my friend, that's all, the one who died. But you're not like him at all."

There was a moment's pause during which my heart sank. I shouldn't have said that, I thought. I had promised myself I wasn't going to say that.

"You must really miss him," Chris said.

"I really do," I said. To my dismay, tears began pouring down my face.

"Good God, Lang, that girl is looking at us again. She's going to think I'm torturing you or something."

"I'm all right," I said, blinking. I could feel the tears I had already shed cold and slightly sticky on my cheeks. It didn't seem fair that crying, on top of the way it hurt, should be humiliating, too.

Chris produced a handkerchief and handed it to me. "Are you all right, now?"

"I'm perfectly fine."

"Liar," he said amiably.

"I'm perfectly fine as long as I don't think about it," I amended.

"I'm a big believer in thinking about it," he said.

"Face up to it? Be a soldier?" I said sarcastically.

"Right. You're better off."

"Depends on what you're facing up to," I said. I sniffled. "Do I look all right? You can't tell I've been crying, can you?"

"You look fantastic," he said. He reached out and put his hand over mine.

I realized then that if I could have waved my straw like a magic wand and replaced Chris with Stu, I might not be missing Stu anymore, but I would be missing Chris. I wanted to wrap Chris up in cellophane and keep him safe so I wouldn't lose him, too.

I knew I had already lost Stu. I couldn't evoke any sense of him now by looking at Chris. Bit by bit I would forget him, forget what he looked like, forget even the timbre of his voice.

"You'll take care of yourself, won't you?" I asked Chris. "To tell you the truth, I don't think I can take losing anything else."

"No suicide planned for today."

"Chris, where are you going to go to college?"

"That's all up in the air," he said, "while my parents fight about it."

"Well, where have you applied?"

"I'd rather not go into it," he said. "I have a kind of superstition. If I count on something and start looking forward to it, I figure that doubles the chances that it's going to blow up in my face. So I try not to expect anything or look forward to anything. Works out pretty well. If I have a motto, it's 'Life is uncertain. Eat dessert first.'"

"That's your philosophy of life?"

"Yep. But you can use it. It's not copyrighted or anything."

"I think I'd have to work out a different one," I said. "It isn't the future that gives me trouble, but what's over and done with."

"I have a plan for that, too," he said. "Want to hear it? I figure you think about it and think about it until you're sick of thinking about it, and then it's over. Kind of like eating hot-fudge sundaes. You eat one hot-fudge sundae you think, 'Great, I could eat ten.' You eat ten, and pretty soon you never want to see another hot-fudge sundae."

"Does it work?"

"Pretty well. I don't go around bursting into tears." I flushed. "I'm sorry."

"Good grief, Lang. You don't have to say that to me. Heck, I don't care if you cry. I mean I care, but it doesn't bother me or anything. Want me to shut up about it?"

"Actually, yes."

"Okay," he said. "I'm shutting up, see?" He clamped his lips together and looked ostentatiously virtuous.

"Okay, so now make one of your wisecracks and cheer me up."

"Funny how when you say that it has a paralyzing effect on my powers of invention," he commented. "Uh, want to go to the prom with me?"

"That's a wisecrack?"

"It's the best I could do on short notice."

"Okay. But I have to warn you, the gym is going to be awash in colored tissue paper fixed up to look like mushrooms and butterflies and stuff."

"I'm tough. I can take it. Hey, I guess this prom thing is something you've got to dress up for."

"Yup."

"I was afraid of that," he said mournfully.

Chapter Nine

Early on prom night I was ironing my slip. I was probably the only girl in Siler Falls who ironed not just her bed sheets but her underwear. I liked the smooth feel of ironed things against my skin. I liked inhaling the steamy heat that rose from the ironing board; I even liked the smell of scorched cotton. If I could have become the literary character of my choice, I would have happily passed up the chance to be Nancy Drew for Mrs. Tiggy Winkle.

I pulled my long, still warm slip off the ironing board and slithered into it, regretting that synthetics and permanent-press items gave the modern-day ironer so little scope. Back in the days of muslin, percale and fine lawn, when dresses were ruched, fluted, gored, tucked and eventually finished off with lace edging, one's skill with the iron could startle and amaze. Now wrinkles were in. I was out of sync with the modern world in my taste for eyelet lace threaded with blue ribbon, for flounces on slips and crisply starched cotton.

What it all came down to, I realized, was that I liked to see signs of care. I loved polished silver, closely shaven lawns and neat flower beds. In that way I was temperamentally different from Stu, who liked excitement, liked to throw and scatter things, liked fireworks. Stu hadn't liked to take care of anything. He hadn't even taken care of himself.

"Do you need any help getting zipped?" Mama said from the door.

"No thanks. I've got it," I said.

In my bedroom I took my dress off its padded satin hanger and stepped into it. The dress was white satin, off the shoulder on one side and had a broad fold of hot-pink satin that ran from the waist to the right shoulder, making it look as if I had been decorated by a foreign government.

"Are you sure you aren't getting dressed too soon?" Mama said, as she turned to head back toward the kitchen. "You've got plenty of time, and you don't want to just sit around trying not to mess up your dress.''

''I hate to rush.''

I could hear Mama's steps as she moved across the parquet floor of the hall toward the kitchen. I opened my drawer to take out a pair of sheer panty hose and saw, next to the neat stack of stockings, Stu's glove.

All at once a memory swept over me so powerfully that the present vanished and suddenly it was the chill March night when I had unexpectedly run into Stu at the mall.

''Lang!'' he had yelled. ''Over here!''

I had been looking at summer straw hats in the window of Ciro's, but at the sound of his voice I wheeled around. When I spotted him I was surprised at how glad I was to see him. I watched him a minute purely for the pleasure of seeing him move. He always held himself well, his chin lifted, as if he were a gazelle or some other wild animal whose life depended on its long sight and its speed. And he walked with the easy, free steps of a mountaineer. Stu had always had the power to awaken images in my mind, to make his simplest movements seem full of hidden significance, with correspondences and connections that ran far beyond the shopping mall.

He strode up to me and grabbed my arm. ''Hey, there,'' he said. ''Are you still speaking to me?''

"Why not?" I asked lightly.

"I have the feeling I was kind of wasted the last time I saw you."

Nobody but Stu would have thought I was still brooding about something that had happened between us seven months before. It annoyed me that he assumed my feelings for him ran so deep that I would still be angry. It annoyed me even more to realize that he was right. I was furious.

"Don't be silly," I said. "You think I've been sitting around all year being mad at you? I've had better things to do."

He smiled at me, and I had the feeling he could tell I was lying. "I'm glad you've forgiven me," he said.

"Why didn't you come home for Christmas, Stu? I thought you would be home then."

"Got an offer to go out to Colorado and ski. You aren't going to hold that against me, are you?"

Yes, I was going to hold it against him. I had been hoping to see him at Christmas so I could make it clear to him how completely detached I had become. I had been very let down when he didn't even show up to give me a chance to demonstrate my indifference. "Skiing?" I said politely. "That's sounds like fun. How are you liking college?"

He shrugged. "Not as bad as high school, but it's still school. I've got Dad's car with me. Want to go for a ride?"

"I don't know. I've got some shopping I need to get done."

"Going to tell me you've got to wash your hair, Lang?" he said derisively. "Let's go. Come along with me. I'm going to stop by a party just for a few minutes. We'll say hello, then we'll get out of there and go someplace, just the two of us. What do you say?"

"All right," I said, weakening. "I guess I would like to hear about college." Why was I doing this? I wondered.

When we were roaring out of the mall parking lot at forty-five miles per hour in second gear, I looked at him uneasily, wondering if he had already had something to drink.

Flip's house was on Tar Valley Lake, less than a mile from Rudene's place, but in a different sort of neighborhood. A number of executives and dentists had built modern houses in the Tar Valley neighborhood, and Flip's house was typical of them, a two-story structure of cedar shingles, with a deck jutting out over the lake and with huge plate glass windows, some tall enough to run all the way from one story to the next. That night, the light was blazing so brightly from all the windows you might have thought the house had been designed as a lantern. Parked cars clogged Flip's driveway and spilled down the street into the darkness. From within the house I could hear an intermittent throb of music.

As soon as we went in the front door, I saw Flip looking a bit unsteady on his feet. "Stu!" he yelled. "Long time no see, huh? Hiya, Lang. Here, let me get you a drink." He gestured with his drink, sloshing some on the carpet. "On second thought," he said, looking down at the dark puddle, "help yourself."

Stu and I went on into the kitchen, and I began methodically opening cabinets, searching for diet cola. I knew that almost every house turned out to have diet cola somewhere, even if it was slightly flat. Eventually, I found some cans of Diet Pepsi at the bottom of the kitchen closet, next to a sack of potatoes.

When I stood up, Stu was pouring Scotch into a tumbler. "Don't you even want any ice?" I asked him, looking at his glass.

"Nah," he said.

I reminded myself that I was not his mother, after all, and I could drive myself home if necessary. Indifference, that was what I should aim at.

Lori Owens came into the kitchen and spotted me with the Diet Pepsi. "Where did you get that?" she screeched. "That's just what I'm looking for."

"Down there by the potatoes."

Lori stooped and began groping around between the bag of potatoes and the bag of onions. "Can you believe this crowd? I haven't seen so many people in one place since the Homecoming game. Hi, Stu," she said, straightening up triumphantly with a Diet Pepsi in each hand. "So you're home on break, now, huh? How do you like college?"

"Okay," he muttered.

I was relieved that he had bothered to speak. He was quite capable of turning his back on people he didn't like and walking away without saying a word to them. On this occasion he did at least bother to deliver the one word to Lori before he turned away and walked out of the kitchen.

"Are you and Stu back together again?" she asked me.

"Goodness, Lori, I've known Stu practically my entire life. I happened to run into him at the mall, and he asked me to come along to the party, that's all."

"I think he is so good-looking," she said, squeezing her eyes closed for an instant. "I had the most terrible crush on him when I was in the ninth grade. Of course, I've grown so much beyond that now, both physically and spiritually. His type doesn't appeal to me at all. I mean, when it comes right down to it, there's something that's really not quite masculine about Stu, wouldn't you say?"

"No," I said coldly. "I wouldn't."

"But he's like a cat. Can't you see it? He's got a green aura. I don't know if I've mentioned that I might be psychic. I'm devoting fifteen minutes a day to getting in touch with my inner perceptions. I feel, like, since I have this gift I owe it to myself to develop it to the fullest." She looked at me with wide open blue eyes. "Tell me, Lang," she said, "do you think Stu is into satanism?"

I choked. "He's an Episcopalian!" I sputtered. I began moving quickly toward the door. "Look, Lori, it's been great talking to you, but I'd better go find Stu."

"No offense, I hope!" she called to my retreating back.

In the living room, Stu had put his drink on the grand piano and was sitting down. I saw him wince, then take his keys out of his pocket and put them on the piano next to his drink. He was wearing his jeans as tight as ever. I slipped a paper napkin under his drink to protect the finish of the piano.

"Don't bother," he said. He picked up his glass and drained the last inch of liquor. "See? All finished." He put the empty glass down on the carpet.

I sat down next to him, looking at him in dismay. "Do you always drink this much?"

He played a few bars of ragtime. "No, sometimes I drink more," he said. "Do you like Scott Joplin? This is from *Treemonisha*."

"*Treemonisha*? That's the name of it?"

"Yeah. It means 'freedom.'" You could tell he loved the word. He was tasting its syllables, as if "freedom" were candy.

I heard the sound of breaking glass from the kitchen and began to wish I were somewhere else. Tinkly notes were pouring from the piano in a jivey rhythm.

A moment later, Tony Roschelli put his hand on Stu's shoulder. The light from the lamp by the piano glinted on his signet ring. "Stu, love," he drawled. "It's been ages."

When Tony, the editor of SFH's literary magazine, had left for Boston University in the fall, he had explained to us all, "I plan to major in degeneracy," and the line hadn't drawn a single laugh. He was tall, willowy, elegant and clever. None of those assets counted for much in Siler Falls, and I'd always wondered if it were because he had spent his life being unfairly despised that he had grown up to be so venomous.

Stu looked up at him with open dislike in his eyes, and I decided to leave so I wouldn't have to watch the inevitable bloodletting. "I was just getting up anyway, Tony," I said, sliding off the bench.

I went in search of a downstairs bathroom. I figured that by the time I returned, Tony would have made his futile overtures to Stu and, with any luck, escaped only slightly scratched from the encounter.

I didn't understand why Tony kept coming around Stu when all he got was rejection. But maybe there was a lesson there for me if I could just see it. What did I get from Stu, if it came to that? It was as if Tony and I hung around for no reason except to warm ourselves at the fires of Stu's beauty and talent. And that wasn't a good enough reason.

I was glad I had decided to cut loose from Stu. It wasn't going to be easy to be indifferent to him. It might take me a while to reach that point. But in a couple of months I would be graduating from high school and going off to college, and in spite of my uneasiness about leaving home, I was beginning to have hopes for myself that I hadn't told to anybody. Lately I had imagined myself coming back to my old high school and thanking my various teachers graciously for the part they had played in launching my career. The exact nature of my brilliant career was not yet clear to me, but I had a growing sense of conviction that whatever I wanted out of life, neither Stu nor Siler Falls played any part in it. It was a frightening idea, one so new and fragile that it needed to be protected in the beginning from critical eyes.

When I found the powder room and opened the door, I heard a clunking sound and looked down to see that the door had hit a bottle of Grand Marnier. The bottle was spinning crazily around on the vinyl. Several empty bourbon bottles stood on the floor and more were up on the counter next to a container of Soft Soap. The smell of bourbon and bitter oranges mingled nauseatingly with pine air freshener. I wrinkled my lip in distaste and bent to gather up the bottles, one by one. Then I kicked the bathroom door open and began moving toward the kitchen. I heard shrill laughter behind me, coming from the stairs at the end of the hall. Considering how wild the entire party was, I suppose it was stupid of me to bother with tidying up the powder room, but I couldn't seem to help myself.

I was by the kitchen door when a loud crash sounded and Madonna's voice became an electronic explosion. Startled, I let one of the bottles slip to the floor. My arms still full of bottles, I tiptoed down the hall a way and looked into the living room. Two guys were sprawled on the remains of the turntable, its plastic cover split in two under them. They seemed to be trying to pull each other's hair, but one of them was impeded by having an arm tangled up in a stereo chord. Relieved to see no one was hurt, I backed up again, picking up the bottle I had dropped, and made my way to the kitchen. The trash container under the kitchen sink turned out to be overflowing with used paper cups, so I neatly stacked the empty liquor bottles next to the Spic and Span and Draino.

When I returned to the living room and looked around anxiously, I saw that a black cord had been ripped out of the wall and lay draped over the shattered turntable. Stu was at the piano again, alone, singing something I could barely hear, and people were beginning to gather around the piano. I leaned against the wall listening to the music, feeling its beat, and thinking how odd it was that a song could seem to echo inside you as if you had meant to sing just that but had never found the notes before. From where I was standing, I couldn't make out the words, but I could hear Stu's voice over the notes of the piano, low and throaty. It was the sort of sound that makes you feel something exciting is hovering over you, ready to burst.

I walked over to the piano and squeezed into the crowd until I could see Stu's shadowed face looking down at the piano keys. I could almost see thought playing across his face, and I wondered if he were making up the words as he went along. He was singing:

"I came home one summer night
To find your heart fire burning bright,

Baby, bring your love to me,
I'll throw it all away-ay,
I'll throw it all away.

"Husks of stars and diamond rings,
And all alive and burning things,
Bring them here to me, babe,
I'll throw them all away-ay,
I'll throw them all away."

He looked up, glancing around at the crowd, and
some trick of the lighting showed a glint in his eye as
he broke into a loud refrain:

"Burning, burning, higher and higher,
Burning, burning, higher and higher,
Moving easy, moving light,
Gonna build a fire tonight—higher."

The last word was a shriek, and I heard an answer-
ing drunken whoop from the other side of the piano.
There was a kind of shudder in the crowd as some of
the boys broke loose and ran out the double doors
onto the deck. The yelling, the shouts of guys daring
each other and threatening each other and the
entreaties of their dates formed the confused background to Stu's reprise of the refrain. Outside, I could
hear splashes as people began diving off the deck.

"Stop it, Stu," I said. "Shut up."

He grinned up at me and sang the last line slowly. Then he stopped playing and leaned back, his eyes bright with mischief.

After a few moments the people standing around the piano began to wander off. I looked behind me and saw Sally Anders bouncing on a chair as if it were a trampoline. She had a preoccupied look, as if she were at the Olympic tryouts for chair bouncing. Behind the chair someone seemed to be throwing up. It was not, I thought, humanity's finest hour.

Stu rose from the piano and put his arm around my waist. I saw that in his other hand was a tumbler half full of amber liquid.

I could hear screams outside, but though I was straining my ears anxiously I couldn't make out any note of panic. I only hoped nobody was getting drowned. "Why did you have to do that?" I said. "What if those guys catch pneumonia? It's freezing out there."

He shrugged. "You think I'm the Pied Piper or something? Get real, Lang. If those guys want to go swimming it doesn't have anything to do with me."

I had the uncomfortable feeling I was making a fool of myself. All he had done was sing a catchy song, after all. It was no crime.

"Come on, let's talk," he said. He downed the rest of his drink, then led me along the hall to the stairway. "Let's go upstairs where we'll have some privacy," he said.

I let go of his hand and sat down on the stairs. "We can talk here," I said. It alarmed me that he had drunk two full tumblers of Scotch, enough to sink anybody on a Breathalyzer test, and I didn't want to be alone in a bedroom with him. But what bothered me more was that he didn't seem to be drunk. Every vowel, every consonant, was as clear as a speech teacher could have wished. He reeked of Scotch, but he was sober. The awful thought occurred to me that maybe he had been drinking so heavily at school that now two tumblers of Scotch were nothing to him.

"What are you doing at school, Stu?" I asked. "Are you studying? Are you keeping up with your music?"

He sat down below me and turned his face up at me. "I don't know. It's rougher than I thought it would be, to tell you the truth. It's hard for me to concentrate, even on the music. I don't know why. I never thought this would happen to me."

"Maybe you just need to work harder," I said. "Are you still keeping your notebooks?"

"I wanted to ask you something about that. I lost them. I left them someplace, or maybe put them in some safe place, but I just can't remember where. I can almost remember, but it won't quite come to me. I think maybe I had a few too many one night, that must have been what happened. Sometimes when I'm drinking I get these kind of blank spots." He hit his knee with his fist. "And now I can't remember. It's driving me crazy. But this is the thing I wanted to ask you. I know a way to get some really good LSD from Mexico, and I thought I might give it a try to see if that would help me remember. What do you think?"

"No," I said quickly. "I'm sure that wouldn't help. It might make it even worse."

"That's what worries me," he said. "I think, what if I freak out and I can't write anymore, you know?" He gave me a look that wrenched my heart. Then he reached for my hand, traces of a smile slowly growing on his lips. "I'm lost without you, Lang. That's what it is."

"Maybe being away from home is just stranger than you thought it would be," I said, withdrawing my hand. "Maybe you depended on your parents more than you thought."

"I don't know. It's weird. Seems like I used to be so sure of what to do. Now I'm just flip-flopping all over the place. I was going to do music. Then I thought maybe film. It's like things won't go into focus for me anymore." He fished a card out of his rear pocket and handed it up to me.

I took it from him and read "Leslie Findlater, M.D., Psychiatrist." At the bottom in smaller print was an Asheville address and a phone number.

"I've been thinking I might give this guy a call," he said, frowning. "What do you think?"

"I'd do it. It can't hurt, and it might help."

"I just wish I could figure out what I did with those notebooks."

He leaned back against the wall, and we sat in silence for a while. I felt so sorry for him I could have burst into tears, but that wouldn't have been much of a comfort to either one of us.

He looked up at me and smiled a little. "Marry me, Lang," he said huskily.

"What did you say?"

"I'm not drunk. Are you thinking I'm drunk? I've never been more sober or more serious in my life. I need you. You can see that. It's always been the two of us, yin and yang. I know I could make it come together if I just had you."

"It wouldn't work," I said. "It could never work."

"I want you, Lang. I need you. What can I say but that?"

"I can't, Stu."

He scrambled up the two steps to sit next to me, and in the panic of the moment all I was conscious of was his breath on my face and the warmth of his body next to mine. I've got to get out of here, I thought.

"Ah, young love," drawled Tony Roschelli from the foot of the stairs. "How nauseatingly sweet."

Stu glared down at him. "You're drunk, Roschelli. Get outa here."

Tony tilted his head winsomely. "Rather a case of the pot calling the kettle black, isn't it, Stuart, my love?"

I squirmed away from Stu and, falling a little way down the steps, squeezed past Tony and ran. I didn't even look back when I heard a thud and a muffled oath from Tony. I ran into the living room, grabbed Stu's keys off the piano and kept going.

When I ran past the kitchen door, I saw Flip sitting slumped against the wall with his eyes closed. Still not looking back, I burst out the front door and ran to Stu's car.

I had no compunction whatever about driving away from the whole mess. Stu would land on his feet. It was myself I had to save.

Chapter Ten

Chris is here," Mama said.

"Chris?" I said stupidly.

"Chris, your date," said Mama, giving me a look.

I jumped up and reached for my evening purse.

"Don't rush off, Lang," said Mama. "Dad wants to get a picture of you and Chris before you leave."

In fifteen years, I had yet to leave for a special occasion without blue spots in front of my eyes. Endless pages of the family album were filled with pictures of me in evening dress, each carefully labeled "4th grade piano recital," "9th grade sock hop," "Holly Ball."

I supposed this one would have to be labeled "12th grade grief."

Chris was standing next to Dad in the living room, barely recognizable in black tie. He had obviously run a comb through his hair in a haphazard kind of way after getting off his bike, and now he had a kind of two-tiered part that changed course midway, his straight hair bristling where the part veered to the right. I would have given a lot to see him tearing down Vine Street in those evening clothes with his red helmet.

"You kids can stand right over there," Dad said, picking up his camera.

I stepped over to the fireplace. This was the backdrop Dad had used for the fifteen previous pictures. He was persistent, but no one would call him original.

"Okay, now, three, two, one—*smile*, Lang." Flash. "I don't think you were looking at the camera. Okay, let's try that again. Look right at the camera. Three, two, one—cheese." A blinding flash went off in my eyes. "I think I'd better reshoot that. I'm not sure you were smiling. Now this time, don't forget to smile." Another flash went off in our faces, and three blue dots danced in front of my eyes. I felt a little dizzy. I hoped I was going to be able to drive.

"Let's try one in the atrium," said Dad.

"We've got to go," I said, firmly grabbing Chris's hand.

"How about just one shot at the door?" asked Dad. I pretended not to hear him and kept moving.

Out in the garage, Chris looked at me and grinned. "He sure does like to take pictures, doesn't he?"

"Yup, my father, the archivist."

We both eased ourselves carefully into the car so as not to crease our clothes.

"Give me your comb," I said. I carefully reparted his hair and began combing it back into place. He kept trying to get a look at himself in the rearview mirror out of the corner of his eye.

"I had a feeling I wasn't quite getting it right," he said.

"There," I said. "That's got it." I laid the comb on the seat, switched on the ignition and began backing out of the garage. "Chris," I said, "I've been thinking about what you said about facing up to things and—well, do you know that poem that goes, '...each man kills the thing he loves'?"

"Nope, and if this is where you pull out a knife and turn into the prom slasher, you can let me out right here."

I looked at him reproachfully.

"Sorry," he said.

I backed out onto the street and began driving up the hill. A moment later we had turned onto Vine. "What I'm wondering is this," I said, "if you do something really bad, do you think you can ever get over it? I'm not talking about something a little bit wrong, but something really big, something you can't undo, something that ended up—well, killing somebody."

"I hope you're going to tell me what you're talking about because I can tell you this little talk is giving me the creeps. What are you supposed to have done that's so awful?"

For a minute or two I couldn't say anything.

"Look, Lang, this is ridiculous. You are a traffic accident waiting to happen. Pull over."

I pulled over into the empty Safeway parking lot. No doubt passersby would take me for an itinerant drug dealer. I didn't care. I was thinking how oddly circular life was. You had this illusion that you were making progress, but you ended up going over the same things again and again, as if your mind were like afternoon television and only played reruns.

"That last night that I saw Stu, he asked me to marry him. And I said no."

"I don't quite get what you're kicking yourself for. Are you thinking you should have said yes?"

"He was falling apart, and all I could think of was how I had to get away from him. I was even thinking that he was bad news. That was practically the last thing I thought about him before I heard what happened."

"This is your friend, right? The one you were telling me about, the one that bought it in a bike accident? Well, not to be blunt about it, but Rudene tells me he *was* bad news."

Tears were streaming down my cheeks. "I wouldn't help him," I said. "I loved him so much, and I wouldn't even help him."

"Good grief, snap out of it, Lang. Here, take my handkerchief. Helping somebody means lending him five bucks, telling him he's got bad breath, cluing him in on what the final was like. It doesn't mean marrying him."

"You don't understand. He was all confused, and he was drinking. He needed me, and I just walked away. And then he drove right into a truck."

"Look, are you thinking Stu went out and got himself drunk and then drove himself into a truck because you turned him down? It's not true. I was there. That pickup turned right in front of him. Nobody on earth could have stopped in time. Evel Knievel couldn't have stopped. The other driver was *charged*, Lang. Don't you read the paper?"

"They charged the other driver?" I said numbly.

"Yeah. It was some real old guy, probably totally gaga, if you ask me. You should have seen him getting out of the truck—he could hardly walk. They shouldn't let people like that drive. I hate to think someday I might meet one of them on the road."

"Stu wasn't even drunk?"

"Well, they usually print the alcohol content of the—" He cleared his throat. "No, he wasn't drunk. Heck, it was the middle of the day."

"You mean it was just an accident that could have happened to anybody?"

"Slow to catch on, aren't you? Yep."

"I guess I hadn't really thought it all out," I said slowly. It hit me that in my headlong determination to avoid thinking about Stu's death, I had never actually asked about the details. I had been so sure of what had happened.

"Feel better now?"

"I guess." It was funny, but I felt a kind of hollow, as if I were losing something important. The guilt I had felt about Stu's death had been a kind of link between him and me, and without it, I felt even more alone.

It was hard to believe that his death had been so random. If that old man had not turned left just then, would Stu be roaring around a corner in that way he had, as if late for a date with destiny, always wild, always drinking too much, always spinning out words and music, throwing his talent away and still having plenty to spare?

"It's so unfair," I cried.

"Life isn't fair," said Chris. "I thought maybe you'd noticed that before. Look, do you want to go to the prom or not? Maybe you'd rather go someplace quiet. We could stop off at an Expressway and get a flashlight and then go out by the reservoir and make out or something."

I looked down at my white dress. "I think we'd better go to the prom. We aren't exactly dressed for the reservoir."

"If you insist," he said cheerfully. "But you're really missing out."

"You are the best friend," I said. My eyes teared up until he was only a blur. "I am going to miss you so much when we all go off to college."

"Don't start crying over *that*, Lang. Give me a break."

"I'm stopping it," I said. I wiped my eyes and hastily put the keys back in the ignition. "See how cheerful I look? How pulled together?" I managed a misty smile.

The prom was in the gym, which was totally unair-conditioned. When Chris and I got out of the car we could almost feel steam rising from our pores. Loud music by the Konks, our home-grown rock band, was pouring out the open doors of the gym.

When we moved inside, I saw that the faces of the dancing couples were glistening with sweat. Eric and Finley danced by us, Finley's pink satin dress sticking to her along the bodice. "Tunnel of love, phooey," Eric snarled at me. "What we need around here is a tunnel of ice."

Chris took my hand, and we began dancing away from Eric and Finley. "Where did Beastie Boy go to charm school?" he said.

"Chris! Lang! Hey!" Rudene and Mike Blackmon were being pressed over in our direction by the surging crowd of dancers. "Can you believe this is our last prom?" said Rudene.

"Don't get Lang started," said Chris, hastily leading me off in another direction.

"I'm okay," I protested. "I'm ready to graduate, Chris, I really am. I want to go off to college. The only thing is, I don't see why a person seems to have to lose so many things. It seems like that's the way the world's made. Do you know what I mean? Every step you take, you lose something. Why is that?"

"I haven't got that figured out, either. And I don't like it much myself."

All around us boys in rented tuxedos danced, sweat streaming down their faces. The girls were sticky in long rustling taffeta gowns and satin dresses with damp circles under the arms. The chaperons sat opposite the punch bowl, a moving electric fan trained on them.

Chris looked around us and shook his head soberly. "Now how could anybody stand to give up all this?" he asked.

Epilogue

Dear Rudene,
College is fantastic, except everybody is so so-
phisticated I can't stand it. The girls all seem to
have Pasts, so I have to pretend that I have a Past
too or I'd feel completely out of it when people
are swapping tales at night around the popcorn
popper. I don't actually *say* anything, of course,
not being really into total fabrication. I just look
mysterious and reserved and concentrate on not
being shocked, no matter *what* anybody comes
out with, which isn't easy.

They just gave us our reading list for Western

Heritage, and I can only suppose it is somebody's idea of a joke because it looks like a photocopy of the Library of Congress card catalogue. However, I am sure that persistence and good study habits will prevail, just the way Miss Smith told us they would.

Last night in the language lab I discovered that the foreign-looking boy in the booth next to mine was listening to an English language tape. "My uncle's ranch has many head of cattle," I heard him say. Then a few minutes later, he said, "I must put up in an inn." Where do they get these scripts, I ask you? But anyway, I went up and got an English tape when I turned in my French one. I got some funny looks, but I didn't let it get to me. I'm working on getting rid of my accent, and by Christmas I plan to sound like Connie Chung. I want to have that spacey, metallic kind of voice that makes you sound as if you were a test-tube baby not born anywhere in particular. I crave to have those hard *r*s, that tiger growl in the middle of words that makes you sound like a world authority.

I have been determined to get rid of my accent since yesterday when my roommate squealed, "I just love the way you say 'thing.' Oh, say it again!" I do not wish to go through life as a sideshow for Yankees. I will still talk to my friends in the same old way, though, so don't worry.

Write, write, write! I am begging and pleading with you. I have no pride left. How do you like Siler Falls Christian? Has anybody new got born in your family, or is the cousin count holding steady? Speaking of cousins, have you heard from Chris? What finally happened with his college? If you have his address, please send it.

I am not very homesick but I am in dire need of letters so that I will have a reason to go on living. Write, or an Egyptian mummy will make your fingernails turn green! Don't think I'm kidding. A sophomore told me she learned this in Asian Civ.

Love,
Lang

I licked the envelope and put a unicorn sticker across the flap. One thing I had learned already at college was that although I had carried a lot of my home away with me in my mind, it didn't seem to do me much good. Mama, Dad, Chris, Rudene and Stu were all as clear in my head as if they were standing before me. But there was no warmth to their images any more than there was warmth in shadows or videotapes. Just thinking about people was no cure for missing them. I missed them all the time, every one of them. Especially Stu, who had gone so much farther away.

When I had told Rudene I was not very homesick, it was a lie, but I had to put up a brave front. I could not have her going to the folks and telling them I was not adjusting properly. I had already put up a calendar in my room and was ticking off the days until Christmas vacation. Seven down and a half million more to go.

The thing I worried most about now was that college was going to change me so much that when I got home I would look around with critical eyes and not even love Siler Falls anymore. Going, going, gone— that seemed to be the theme song of my life.

"Are you going to mail that?" asked Cindy. "Could you mail mine, too?"

My roommate's dyed black hair sat in sculpted spikes over her soft white face. It took her ten minutes in the morning to put on her eyelashes alone. If I had seen her in Siler Falls I would have known just what to think, but one week in college had taught me that it would probably be better to suspend all judgment for the first semester at least.

"Sure," I said. I took her envelope and walked out of the dorm into the bright sunshine. I wondered when I was going to be able to think about all the people I

loved without feeling as if I were about to die of lone-
liness. Sometimes I felt like lifting my chin mournfully and howling like a dog. Probably the only thing
that stopped me from doing it was the knowledge that
it would have caused a sensation in the dorm.

I was walking on a close-shaven lawn that was dap-
pled with sun and shadow. The lawns of the college,
together with the ivy-covered halls, had been a big
factor in my final decision on where to go to school,
but already I was noticing some difference between
what I had imagined it all would be like and the real-
ity. Judging from the college brochure, for example, I
would have guessed that fully half of the classes were
held out under a tree on a sunny day, with a lake
sparkling in the background. So far, however, my
professors had shown a decided preference for holding classes in classrooms.

But the lawns had their uses. Now, as I trudged
across a broad green expanse of Bermuda grass, I saw
a student sprawled on his stomach near a tree, reading. If the crimson cover were any clue, I judged he
was reading the most daunting book on the humani-
ties reading list, Plato's *Republic*. The very sight of
that thing had made me start thinking of using Cliffs
Notes, something I had thought I would never sink to.

I noted wistfully that the boy on the lawn looked
like Chris. After a week at college, I had become used

to that phenomenon. The unconscious part of my mind had not yet figured out that I had left Siler Falls. It kept looking for familiar faces even though there were none to be seen. I was always beginning to smile at someone and then realizing that he was a perfect stranger.

"Lang!" he yelled, scrambling to his feet.

It was Chris. It really was. I started running.

"Watch out," he said. "You've dropped your letters."

"I don't care," I said. I threw my arms around him and squeezed hard.

He grinned and hugged me back. "I'm glad to see you, too," he said.

"Why didn't you tell me you were coming here?"

"Life is uncertain, remember? I was afraid if I told you, it would put a hex on it and I'd never make it."

"Well, you've made it," I said, feeling the satisfaction seep into some of the sad cracks of my heart. "How's Plato's *Republic*?"

"Very interesting," he said, sitting down on the grass. "I read it on several levels, you know. There's the political angle and the philosophical level, then—"

"Chris, have you got the Cliffs Notes?"

He looked offended. "Certainly not. All this comes from my first-class brain."

I had to admit I was impressed.

"Plus the introductory notes," he added thoughtfully.

I sat down next to him and punched him lightly in the stomach. It was nice to think that not everything had to get itself lost. Some things turned up again, like lucky pennies. And like Chris. "I must put up at an inn," I said in my most hoity-toity voice.

"Whahh?"

"I'm practicing on losing my accent," I said proudly.

"Why would you want to do a thing like that?" he said.

"Well, it's this way. I want to sound like—"

He put his arm around me, drew me close and kissed me. I reminded myself that now that I was in college I could never be called into the office and reprimanded for public displays of affection, so I kissed him back.

We sat there companionably for a minute, holding hands. I was beginning to have the feeling that I could be happy at college. Not even putting my teddy bear on my dresser had given me quite the same comfortable feeling that the sight of Chris had.

"I was going to write you," I said. "I just asked Rudene to send me your address."

"Gee, I hate to disappoint you, Lang," he said. "I know what a kick it is to get mail around here."

I punched him in the stomach again.

"Ouch," he said, pretending to writhe in agony. "I think you've hit my old war wound."

"Don't worry," I said, grinning at him. "I'd much rather have you than a letter."

* * * * *

The Basic Pedicure

1. Wash your feet in the bath or in a basin of warm soapy water.

2. Soak about five minutes.

3. Work up a lather and scrub rough heel areas with a pumice stone, loofah or washcloth. Remove dead skin cells and wake skin up!

4. Dry feet thoroughly with a thick towel, especially between the toes.

5. Apply a moisturizer all over feet, especially on heels, which tend to be dry.

6. Sprinkle on a little powder or cornstarch to help stem foot odor and perspiration. (Your feet have 250,000 sweat glands and can give off as much as half a pint of perspiration a day.) But don't go overboard with the powder—pouring an entire container on your foot will cause caking and may eventually lead to infection.

7. Cut toenails straight across. Do not try to file or shape.

8. If you like, paint your toenails a fashionable color. They'll look very pretty with open-toed sandals or barefoot at the beach. Paint toenails the same way you paint fingernails.

**How do you break up with a sweet guy like Ernie?
As Amy soon finds out,**

IT ISN'T EASY!

For a good laugh, read

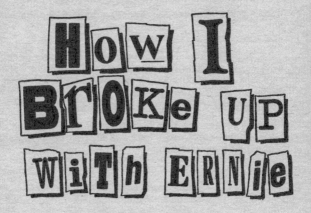

HOW I
BROKE UP
WITH ERNIE

by R.L. Stine

Available from Crosswinds in September

COMING NEXT MONTH
FROM
CROSSWINDS™

THE HOUSE WITH THE IRON DOOR
by Margaret Mary Jensen

April was determined to find the cause of her grandfather's mysterious death. Was the answer behind the iron door?

FROG EYES LOVES PIG
by James Deem

At the top of Allan's list was, *Get a girlfriend*. But first he had to change his image. It wouldn't be easy.

AVAILABLE THIS MONTH

THE BLACK ORCHID
Susan Rubin

STU'S SONG
Janice Harrell

COMING NEXT MONTH
FROM
Keepsake

KEEPSAKE # 29
MASQUERADE
by Janice Harrell

Finally Ann-Marie's dream guy had asked her for a date.
She should have realized that it was too good to be true.

KEEPSAKE # 30
SPRING BREAK
by Bebe Faas Rice

A hilarious sequel to *Boy Crazy*. Portia and her ditzy
roommates are on the prowl again. Their prey: BOYS!

AVAILABLE THIS MONTH

KEEPSAKE # 27
BOY CRAZY
Bebe Faas Rice

KEEPSAKE # 28
GETTING IT TOGETHER
Anne Ferguson

Little extras you'll love . . .

In the next few months we'll be bringing you some important tips about hair, nails, makeup . . . everything you need to know to look good!

**How to care for your skin
Makeup do's and don'ts
The perfect hairstyle for you
Beauty quizzes . . .
            and much more.**

Watch for these extras from now on . . .
   in Keepsake and Crosswinds books.